Zona

Investigations: The

918 Files

Case #Gilbert00017

Jason Cvancara

I CAME, I SAW, I'M NOW CREEPED OUT...

i

Dedication

Dedicated to those "thought" to be crazy

CONTENTS

About the Author

Jason Cvancara was born in Fargo, North Dakota, but grew up all over the United States and Europe as his father served in the Air Force.

After high school, he enlisted in the Air Force, where he discovered his love for law enforcement as a Security Forces member. Once his enlistment was over, he moved to Arizona, became a police officer, and eventually started his own private investigation business.

As an author, he combines experiences from his career in law enforcement and the military with his creative mind to create stories that will keep you guessing whether what you are reading is fiction or reality.

Preface

Gilbert00017, a case so strange, nobody believed it. A man was found lying in the street with bruises and scratches all over his body.

In 1918, at 6:10 pm, Harry ran and ran, thinking he could escape the mess that he was sucked into. He had lost all hope when finally, he saw the light but little did he know that he wasn't just in the wrong place but also the wrong era.

Charles believed him when nobody else did. Charles G. William and his private detective agency, "Zona Investigations," was developed for the ones desperate to find answers.

Intense drama, mysterious details combined with doubtful eyes; will anyone believe Harry? Will he be able to prove his innocence, or will he end up choosing silence over proving himself?

Introduction

"When you're young, you think you're invincible."

Everyone hears that line at some point in their lives from the second they're old enough to get into trouble. Stealing your parents' car, skipping class at school, or sneaking out to a party where you can walk up to anyone, name a drug of your choice, and you'll have some in your hands in a matter of minutes.

And let's be honest – up to a certain age, you truly feel invincible. You're healthy, full of energy and ambition, and you've got the most robust mind you'll ever have. There's no denying that.

And then one day, after you've checked all the boxes off your list – get married, buy a house, have kids, land a stable job – you find yourself slowing down.

It starts small. You'll forget your keys in the lock after coming home from a long day at the office. You get to the grocery store and realize you left the list at home. Once

1

in a while, you'll momentarily forget your kids' names and mix them up, calling one by the other's name.

But then, instead of it happening once a month, it starts happening once a week. Once a day. And soon, you're trying to unlock someone else's car, convinced that it's your own.

As a teenager, I truly believed I would never get old. How could I? I was captain of the baseball team, leading my team to a championship after championship. I wasn't at the top of my class, but I did well across the board and garnered high praises from my teachers. There was nothing Dr. Pepper couldn't get me through.

After I graduated high school, I decided that college wasn't the right place for me. I had an abundance of energy that I knew could be put to better use. I wanted to do something impactful with my life – something that would let me leave my mark in history. So, at the ripe age of 18, I enlisted in the Air Force.

For better or worse, being in the military was not as they made it out to be in the movies. There was no ongoing war, I wasn't deployed to a nation troubled with poverty and violence, and my day-to-day was surprisingly normal. In fact, I only got a couple of hours of airtime a year. But it had structure and support – something that helped to tame my haywire mind.

I ended up in the security forces realm, and working with my supervisors, I had shown a knack for identifying points of weakness and plugging holes into the security gaps. Over the years, which was a mix of active duty and reserves, I rose from a young, slick sleeve to a non-commissioned officer to a senior non-commissioned officer, and eventually, I was promoted to Chief. With a coffee almost always in one hand and orders from my overstressed commanders in the other, I learned more than I could've ever imagined when I enlisted at 18-years-old.

It was, in fact, in the Reserves that I met Jamie. A sharp soul with even more sharp eyes, she was serving as a nurse, and we'd run into each other on occasion when we'd mingle with other departments. Her dark brown hair caught my eye, and soon after, I caught hers. Like all great love stories, the rest is history.

As with all jobs, the urge to move on to something

new came over me. I realized that I had garnered all the knowledge that I possibly could, and I wanted more. Jamie and I, now married, felt that it was time to settle our lives.

After eight years of active duty, I left the Air Force. We moved into Phoenix, ready to return to civilian life, engorged in the Arizona heat surrounded by the scattered landscapes.

Jamie decided to take some time off as we decided to start our family – as excited as she had always been about her nursing career, she was even more excited to be a mother. By nature, she was attentive and caring and made up for my disheveled mind.

As the next phase of our life began, I pursued the next natural career path – I joined the City of Phoenix police department. I spent the first few years getting my hands dirty as a street officer, working various duties, and responding to minor crimes. Slowly but surely, I worked my way up to more serious crimes, supporting detectives in my precinct as I studied to earn my own detective certification. Inside the steel-gray walls of the police station, with the aroma of burnt coffee seeping its way into the ever-increasing piles of paperwork, I spent hours pouring over unsolved cases, trying to put the missing pieces together.

The military experience put me ahead of the game, and I was detective certified sooner than you could blink. But the monotony and red tape of the police force became frustrating – I felt stunted in my career, and the thrill I sought out was left unfulfilled. I resigned after ten years of hard, grunt work and thought about what to do next.

The idea came to me on a scorching summer day. Temperatures had been higher than I could even remember. In fact, I think that was the year they discovered that eggs could be fried on the roads of Arizona.

I sat at my kitchen counter, donning my old but trusted sweat pants and brown military t-shirt, with the ceiling fan running at full speed as we tried to keep the heat off our skin. My wife stood over the stove, wearing her favorite blue apron I had bought her for a birthday some years prior, putting together an elaborate breakfast for the kids, as she always did on Saturday mornings.

Laid out all over the counter were business plans for my own coffee brewery company, a side hobby I'd been planning in my time of unemployment. I was known for always having a freshly brewed cup of coffee in my hand at any given point in time, so I thought, why not capitalize on it.

Our most cherished member of the family, Duke – a 70 pound German Shepherd with fur that made Jamie envious and a need for attention more pertinent than our toddler – was nuzzled up against my feet, just waiting for the first sign of crumbs falling from above. I'd had a lot of partners in my lifetime, but Duke was surely the most loyal of them all.

The scent of the sizzling bacon wafted across the house, and like puppies hearing the sound of a bag of food being shaken in the next room, four sets of feet came tumbling down the stairs and into the kitchen. Duke lept up to his feet to join the kids in their excitement for the day ahead. I remember this day vividly, not only because I was about to journey off into what was the most fascinating portion of my career, but because, despite the constant sweat dripping down our backs, it was a simply perfect day. Those don't come around too often.

I thought about how over the last 11 years I'd been serving, whether the military or the police force, I had been working in tandem with an established system, curving my practices to match theirs and following the rules to a tee.

Now that I had seen that side of the aisle, I wanted to take a walk on the other – I wanted to make the rules. So as I stood in the kitchen, my family chattering over pancakes and eggs, I decided to start my own business.

I wanted to help others. I thought about the days I sat in the precinct till ungodly hours, flicking the pages of cold case files, wondering – who was still trying to help these people? So many dead ends left in the shadows because there wasn't enough budget or too many hoops to jump through. Someone ought to help them – and so I did.

In the spare room of our humble house, I cleared out the dust and cobwebs to make way for what would become my office. A week later, after a trip to Walmart and a rummage through the toolkit, I set up the essentials – a desk, internet, a phone connection, and my trusted Keurig, which I stole from the kitchen. And there I spent the next 30 years, working case after case, trying to solve what seemed to be a never-ending string of unexplainable instances.

I never thought it would be me. I suppose no one ever does. But as I strolled around the West Creek Senior Citizens home close to our home in Gilbert, accompanied by my daughter Lilly and my fluffy sidekick Duke, as they showed me the various amenities and services, I thought to myself – this is really happening. I've reached the final stage of my life.

You may think I was being overdramatic, and perhaps I was. Age is a scary thing, but we all know it's coming. It is, after all, the natural progression of life.

The tour guide was a chirpy young man, likely in his mid-30s. He wore a pastel-blue polo shirt, the top button open with a darker lanyard hanging around his neck. "Joshua Willis," his ID card said. His hands continued to make their way in and out of the pockets of his khaki shorts, which fell just above his knees, as he waved them occasionally to point out yet another service that was supposed to make me feel right at home. "Best of all, we are 100% pet friendly," he said, smiling down at Duke.

Just like Joshua's shorts – which was what all the

boys seemed to be wearing these days – all this tour did was make me feel older than I already did. And I felt pretty damn old.

Lilly meant well. She was the second of four siblings, and despite not being the group leader, she certainly was the most caring and kind-hearted. Maybe sometimes too much.

Growing up, she had always taken things to heart. When a classmate didn't show up to her 6th birthday party, she nagged her mother until she called the parents to figure out why little Drew wasn't able to come and enjoy the bouncy castle. It turned out he just had a cold, but she had to make sure. At Lilly's request, we sent over her handmade get-well-soon card and some chicken noodle soup.

By the time she was in her teens and her older sister, Megan, went off to college, she had mastered the art of being the oldest sibling in the house. One week, rumors began to float that my youngest son, Hunter, was being picked on. She marched on over from the senior crowd at the bleachers during a high school football game and had a conversation with the freshman that had been tormenting her little brother. To this day, we have no idea what she said to him, but he never bothered Hunter – or anyone – ever again.

Lilly had flourished into a strong, firm woman, just like her mother. Her husband worshipped the ground she walked on, and her kids looked up to her as their hero. In all her glory, she was still my little girl and spent every Sunday afternoon on my porch listening to me complain about politics, each of us with a cup of coffee in hand. She might have had her mother's wit and her hair color, but her taste buds definitely came from me.

After my wife Jamie passed away, Lilly became increasingly worried about my well-being – with reason, I suppose. Loneliness can be more brutal than they say.

While my wife and I had had our own routines, they were closely intertwined with one another. I brewed my morning coffee while she cracked the eggs into the pan, sprinkling in our favorite cheese and sausage. I went off to work, and she walked over to the local library to volunteer as a guide. I worked late while she sat on the couch adjacent to me – Duke alternating between our laps for his evening nap – and read her choice of supernatural fiction for the night. After I retired, we spent our days reminiscing over the days of our youth and planning our next family trip with our grandchildren. So when she was gone, my routine didn't change, but it surely was not the same.

Somewhere along the way, the confusion started. As I made my morning coffee the way I had for the past 70 odd years, I would forget to put the coffee cup at the base of the machine. I would go out looking for the morning paper in my front yard, only to come back into the house and realize I had already picked it up an hour earlier. I'd pour food into Duke's bowl more times than was necessary in one day. Poor guy gained 10 pounds due to no fault of his own.

On more than one occasion, I strolled my shopping cart of groceries over to my car, and after a few attempts to unlock the trunk and a short argument with the owner, I realized it was, in fact, not my car.

Then, one morning, I woke up, picked up the phone, and dialed Lilly, asking if her mother had gone over to her place for breakfast. She called the nursing home the same day.

"See, dad, it isn't so bad, right?"

I looked over at Lilly as she stared back at me with my own stark hazel eyes. My gaze then shifted to the resident bedroom – blue-gray walls, almost like the ones at the police precinct, stared back at me, adorned with generic framed photos of the ocean.

To the left, the wooden bed frame was tucked into the corner, laid out with crisp floral bedding, accompanied by a matching table hosting a small lamp, a resident tablet, and a copy of the Bible. You'd think they'd just download a copy onto the tablet for the sake of saving paper.

Across the bed was a desk placed neatly under the window, which overlooked the nursing home garden. Numerous folks shuffled around, some with walking sticks, others accompanied by visitors. I thought – is that what I look like?

The two love seats against the right wall and an adjoined bathroom summed up the simple bedroom. It had everything an older person needed – a place to sleep, a place to sit, and a place for visitors.

I looked down at Duke as he stared back up at me as if to say, "Really? This place?" I suppose it would have to make do.

Later that day, I asked Lilly to take me to my office – the back corner of our family home, out of which I'd started my private investigation services. The nursing home wouldn't have space for all this, so I'd have to figure out what I wanted to keep and what could be tossed out or donated.

I rarely went in there anymore. I'd retired almost ten years ago, worn out by the array of cases I'd put my mind to work for. Sometimes I wondered if I worked too much – Jamie would often tell me I did. But she knew how much I loved the work and how good I was at it. So she never pushed me to stop, only to take a break now and then.

I ran my fingers over the edge of the desk, feeling the cracks that had formed over the years from the weight of files, books, and miscellaneous papers. A smooth layer of dust had formed over the top of the piles – I almost didn't want to disturb it. It felt like an ancient artifact that, if tampered with, could be damaged forever.

I grabbed a random folder off the corner and wiped off the dust for a clearer look. "Zona Coffee Company." I held in a soft laugh – the company that had never gotten off its feet. Working hours on end, day and night, I never had the time to make this dream a reality. Perhaps I'd hand the idea off to one of my grandkids to carry on my legacy.

"Grandpa, why do you have so much stuff? What is all this?"

I turned my head around as a smirk crept over my face, looking over at my grandson, Brady. He had a lost expression on his face, his nose wrinkled and brows furrowed like he couldn't quite get along with the musty smell that had accumulated over the years.

"Stories, my boy. These are stories."

File 918

Brady was like any other 8-year-old, for the most part.

A third-grader with the chatter of a teenager, Brady was the most adventurous of all my grandkids. In fact, he reminded me a lot of myself.

Since the day he took his first steps, he's been a fiery presence in Lilly's household. Crawling into any and every space he could, grabbing things he shouldn't, just trying to figure out what they were, and attempting to sneak out of the front door into the unknown world every chance he got. He certainly didn't make life easy for his parents, but he had the kind of spirit every child should have.

A few years ago, Lilly would get a call from Brady's teacher at least once a week. The first few times, she'd sped through traffic – even getting a ticket on one occasion – worried that something had happened to her little boy. She'd arrive to find out that Brady had fought another child over their brand-new toy or taken a book from the teacher's desk without permission.

Anything he could get his hands on that he hadn't seen before, he couldn't resist the urge to take for himself. He'd say that he "just wanted to know what it was." Yet, even in such a simple manner, he expressed curiosity everywhere he went.

After a few incidences of the same nature, instead of speeding, Lilly would take her time, pick up a coffee on the way, and stroll down the pale tile floors into the school, knowing exactly what her meeting with his teacher was going to look like. She'd accepted her son's enthusiasm and even learned to embrace it – and even encourage it. She had a feeling that one day, his curious mind would take him places.

Because of his interest in any and every new thing, we couldn't keep Brady interested in one thing for very long. As soon as he'd figured out the functions of one new toy, he'd get bored and immediately start looking for the next. His scattered brain emanated mine, and for that, I would apologize to Lilly often, joking that unfortunately, he might grow up to be like his grandfather instead of his father.

Brady was Lilly's youngest child. He had a sister, Emily, who was just two years older than him. She was spirited like her mother but had a calmer soul and a well-mannered demeanor. While her brother was flying around the house like a tiny hurricane, she'd be teetering on a step stool next to her mother at the kitchen counter, desperate to help make the night's dinner.

While on opposite ends of the personality spectrum, sometimes you couldn't tell the two apart by just looking at them. Both had thick ringlets that fell into their eyes, courtesy of their father, and each had a slightly varying shade of green in their eyes. That was from my Jamie.

When their grandmother passed away, the kids were just old enough to understand what had happened but young enough that they couldn't fully process the situation. "How can grandma be gone? She was just here?" they'd ask. You'd think between myself, their parents, and several aunts and uncles, someone would be able to handle the confused toddlers asking where their grandmother was. It was easier said than done.

Jamie had loved to spoil our grandkids. From the moment Emily was born, the first of the lot, Jamie was ready with clothes, shoes, accessories – anything that you could possibly imagine a baby girl would need, she'd gotten it. Once she'd started, she could not be stopped.

After Jamie was gone, I couldn't bear to leave the kids without the love and affection she showed them, so I did my very best to take over as the favorite grandparent. However, the closest I could get to it was taking Emily for ice cream dates to her favorite spot in town and bringing Brady replicas of the latest Air Force gadgets. I even tried to get them interested in coffee like I was – that was before I was adamantly scolded by my own daughter that toddlers had no business trying different strains and brews of coffee.

As it turned out, Brady and I didn't need coffee to form our special bond. With his father's long working hours, whenever Lilly required to run errands or spend some time by herself, Emily would be dropped off at a friend's house, and Brady would be with me.

Brady knew I'd been in the Air Force and the police

force, and he'd taken a particular interest in fighter jets. Lucky for him, I kept in touch with several of my old Air Force buddies, who would catch me up on the latest technology and weaponry.

I'd tell Brady stories from my days of service, adding in some embellishments to make them more exciting – I suppose to make him feel like he had a cooler than average grandfather. While we played with the toy jets I'd gotten him for Christmas one year, I'd tell him all about the new state-of-art planes that my colleagues were flying and training in – all their features, their speeds, and where they'd be traveling.

I knew Brady was a special kid because even as a toddler, he'd memorize all the specs of the jets I'd tell him about and repeat them back to me the next time we'd see each other. Even his teacher, despite his classroom antics, was thoroughly impressed by a show and tell presentation where he talked his classmates' ears off about all the different types of jets he'd learned about.

Standing in my old office, Brady's figure appeared lankier and taller than I remembered. That's one of the things they don't tell you about growing old – for all the years you grew, you would start to shrink as you age, your back turning downward like a wilted plant.

He ruffled his dark brown hair as he continued to look around my dim office space. No doubt, he'd be wondering why his grandfather would've kept all this junk. As frivolous as I was, I could still maintain my focus. Kids these days become infatuated with one thing – the latest gadget, app, or video game – only to move onto something else the very next day. They didn't have the same value for history and preservation as we did.

"This stuff is so old, grandpa. You should throw it out and get new stuff. Mom just got me the latest iPad, and it's SO cool!"

I had to resist the urge to roll my eyes at my beloved grandson.

"Kid, back when I was your age, we actually had buttons on all our gadgets! And they worked just fine too." That, of course, was a bald-faced lie. I couldn't deny the leaps and bounds made by technology in improving the way the world works. I was in the Air Force after all – I saw the world change right before my very eyes. But I'd never let the kids think they were the faster generation!

"So why are we here, grandpa?"

"Well, kid, you know grandpa isn't going to live in this house much longer, and my new place isn't going to have much space. So, unfortunately, as you so kindly suggested, I am going to have to pack up a lot of this stuff. I just don't have the heart to throw it out – this is my life's work after all."

And it was. After all the career switches I had made in life, I knew that private investigation was my true calling. Being able to do the work that I was good at but not be stuck in a rut of a boring routine because every case was different and challenging. The thrill of tracing down a lead, camera in one hand and notepad in the other, was unmatched. And when I finally cracked a case – oh man, there was nothing like that feeling of success and the gratitude from your client for helping them solve their mystery.

To my little Brady, in his world of electronics and gadgets, all of this may have looked like old, useless paperwork. But to me, it was the archive of my 30 years of hard work. It was my proudest possession. I'd never say that to Lilly, though.

"Alright, kid, what are you doing standing around? Put those skinny arms to use and start packing stuff up!"

Little Brady let out an audible huff but made no further complaints and pulled one of the cardboard boxes out of the corner that was almost bigger than him. If he wasn't careful, he'd get packed in with all my things.

I didn't miss the fact that with every file or paper he'd pick up, he would flip through pages before gently setting it down into the box.

It then occurred to me that not only was he too young to possibly understand the details of those case files, but that he did not know the extent of the work I had done for most of my life.

I'd have loved to share more of my private investigation work with my family – it would have been like their real-life crime show. But aside from client confidentiality, not every case was simple and clean cut. There were times when I had gotten myself into some close calls and uncomfortable situations. Of course, I'd never told anyone about it because they'd only worry. And well, the kids were too young to hear such stories.

As a private investigator, the cases brought to me by clients were different than what you'd see at a police station or the likes. When people came to a private investigator, much of the time, what they wanted to be investigated was either something the police could not help them with or something they didn't want the police to know. As part of the contract, I was required to keep the investigation between myself and the client – it would not go beyond the walls of my office. So it worked out in their favor.

Low mumbling from Brady brought me out of my nostalgic train of thought. I looked over my shoulder to see him swiping dust off a tub in the far corner of the room, lifting the lid off so he could bring it closer and read the label.

His scrunched-up face told me he was struggling to read what was written – that was likely attributed to my illegible handwriting. Like my mind, my hand was quick, and as long as I understood what it said, that was all that really mattered.

I began to walk in his direction when he managed to decipher the label.

"Files… 918… Grandpa, what's 918?"

918. I hadn't thought about that number in so long that I almost didn't register what Brady was talking about. That tub had indeed been gathering dust for years, tucked away in a corner where I wouldn't see it too often. Out of sight, out of mind, as they say.

At that moment, my first instinct was to put the lid back onto the tub, shut it tight and never open it again. But I realized that by keeping it away, I'd be ignoring some of the most incredible cases I'd ever worked on – the ones that brought me some of the greatest experiences of my life. And who better to share that with than my own prodigy?

So I decided not to put the tub away. Instead, I asked Brady to drag it over to the desk, where I took a seat in my old chair – the one I'd spent most hours of my life on, studying clues and analyzing leads.

He brought the tub over, and he dropped down to the

floor into a cross-legged position, almost instinctively, like he knew I was about to tell him a story. He looked up at me with those familiar green eyes, as he had so many times before, in anticipation of what I would say next. The story I was about to tell him; he would surely never forget.

#Gilbert00017

There's something about mysteries that get people riled up. Some people love the thrill of not knowing what's going to happen next. Others enjoy easy mysteries because they can pick up on the clues and figure out what's going to happen by the time they turn the page. And more often than not, we use mysteries and thrillers as a way to escape from our own realities and jump into one that is more exciting.

When I think back on my years of private investigations and all the memorable cases I encountered, I wonder – was it more than just a job?

There were so many cases where the accounts, the clues, the people that I came face to face with, were out of this world. I would be so caught up in trying to find answers that everything would be put on the back burner – all I could think about was solving the mystery. So I suppose it was more than just a job – it was an escape.

Jamie hated those cases, and she could immediately

tell when I was about to go down the rabbit hole. I'd skip dinners, even when she'd cook my favorite meal. Sometimes she'd jokingly set a plate outside the door of my office, hoping the smell would waft through the cracks and lure me out of my daze.

I'd stay awake till all odd hours of the night, searching through papers and tapping away in online search engines for explanations for the bizarre occurrences my clients would bring to me. I'd sneak my way into the kitchen for yet another cup of coffee.

Some nights, I just had an insatiable craving for freshly ground coffee – there's just nothing like it. I'd gently swing open the kitchen cupboards, pull out my coffee beans, and would try my best not to wake Jamie up from the crackling sounds of the coffee grinder.

Some cases also required me to travel. Clients would contact me from different towns, even other states, so distraught with their situations that when detectives or police near them couldn't help, they decided to outsource.

I tried my best to cover all my bases from home, but it was difficult to crack a case when the clues and leads were miles away. That and the fact that some clients were insistent that I visit them in person. So I'd drive or fly out to their localities and start working the case from there.

Jamie and I would always argue when I was about to go on these trips.

"Why can't you just take cases that are here at home? You're barely ever home now," she'd say to me as I was packing away my things into a creaky old suitcase. I'd always been too stubborn to pay for a new one.

"Jamie, sweetheart, these people came to me because no one else can help them. This is what I do best – how can I say no?"

She'd give me the cold shoulder for days after I returned – but she was no where near as bad as Duke. He, who on any regular day would not leave my side and loved me unconditionally, held a grudge worse than any human I'd ever met.

When I'd walk through the door upon my return from yet another work trip, instead of his usual greeting – running right up to me and lifting his upper body into the air for a hug – I'd be met with the cold shoulder. He'd look up at me from across the room before silently turning his gaze away and snuggling up next to Jamie's feet as she sat in her armchair. It'd take days of treats for him to warm up to me again.

"C'mon, grandpa, we don't have all day! What's the story about?"

I let out a hearty laugh. Brady was definitely my grandson – impatient as ever to get things done and over with.

As bright as he was, he was young enough to only know the details of my work in the Air Force and the police department. What we'd told him his whole life was that even after I stopped being a police officer, I still was a detective – which wasn't a complete lie; it simply wasn't the whole truth.

Lilly had wanted to keep Brady sheltered for as long as she could. She believed that children deserved to keep hold of their innocence and their childhood when they were younger. For this reason, she'd asked me not to talk about my cases in front of Brady for fear that he'd start to ask too many questions.

"The world is a dark place," she'd say. "But he doesn't need to know that yet."

So instead, when Brady would ask me questions about my work, why I was gone for weeks at a time, and why I spent so much time in the office, I'd keep my answers as vague as possible. I'd simply tell him I was helping people solve their problems.

But now, as I was settling into the final stages of my life, who knew how much more time I had left with my grandson. As I looked down at him, his green eyes staring back at me, anticipating what I was going to say next, I couldn't contain the excitement just thinking about how much he'd love the mysteries of the 918 files. And I thought, maybe one day, he'd tell his own children the stories of his grandfather's adventures.

"So kid, you remember how I was a detective for a long time, right?"

"Yeah, grandpa – I told all my friends too! You solve

crimes like a superhero."

I smirked. "I sure did, but crimes weren't the only things I solved."

An adult-like perplexed expression took over Brady's young face.

"What do you mean? What else did you do?"

With that, I began to tell Brady more about my work.

I tried my best to explain private investigation in the simplest terms, making sure not to throw too much information at the kid all at once. I'd sure be hearing it from Lilly afterward, so the least I could do was take it slow.

"So, you know how detectives find clues to try and solve crimes, searching for the culprit? Well, sometimes the police can't solve the case – especially the difficult ones. They can't spend too much time on one case because then all the other cases get ignored. And sometimes, the police don't believe people when they report a... situation."

"Okay… but then what happens to those cases?"

"Good question, my boy. So when the police can't solve a case, or when a person doesn't want to report something to the police, they have to find other people to help them figure out what happened. That's where private investigators come in."

"Private investigators… okay. So they're not police. Do they work for the government?"

"They do not. In fact, they don't work for anyone. They work for themselves. Do you remember how I would spend all that time in my office? That's because I worked for myself."

"Oh, okay. I get it… I think. But grandpa, how do people find you if you don't work for anyone?"

Ah, and the questions keep on coming. That was another thing about the private investigation – establishing yourself as a reputable business.

"Well, at first, it's pretty difficult. You have to start with the small, easy cases and build a reputation for yourself. Once you've worked for a couple of years, people start to know your name and hear about how you're good at solving cases. So they come to you for help. You have to make sure people know you're good at your job!"

"Hmm… that sounds difficult, grandpa. Why did you do that? Why didn't you just stay with the police?"

"Sometimes, people are just better working on their own than working with a team."

Brady looked like he was deep in thought. He scrunched up his brows as he pulled the lid off the 918 Files tub and started running his hands over the numerous folders that were in the box. He stopped at one and pulled it out, instinctively brushing the dust off with his hands.

I saw the file he'd pulled out and said, "Oh boy, that's a good one right there, son."

"Really? What's it about?"

"You know how I said sometimes the police can't solve cases? Well, that's because some cases don't make much sense at first. In fact, you see all those files in there? In a lot of those cases, the police turned these people away.

When they said what happened to them, they just didn't believe them."

"Oh boy, really? Did they see ghosts or something?!"

I let out a hearty laugh. But the funny thing was, Brady wasn't that far off.

"Close, kid, you're pretty close. Anyway, when the police didn't take them seriously, they became desperate for anyone who could help them find answers to what happened to them. And that's when they came to me. Let me see what you got there."

He passed the file over to me, and I flipped it open. Specs of dust flew up from the pages as I turned over through the various notes, clues, and emails I'd collected during this case.

"Brady, before I start telling you the story, I have to warn you, you're gonna think your old man is crazy. Heck, I thought I was crazy back then too!"

"I don't think you're crazy, grandpa."

"I sure hope not!"

In this particular case, Gilbert 00017, even I almost couldn't believe the story. At first, I didn't believe it at all. But that's the thing about private investigation – you have nothing to lose.

Harry is one of the most persistent clients I've ever had the pleasure of working for. In his defense, he had to be. Otherwise, no one would've ever looked into his case.

I envision Harry as a young professional, maybe around 25, works in an office, moved to Arizona about 3 years ago after graduating from the University of Minnesota with a business degree, sports fan (huge fan of Minnesota sports teams), and is seen as someone who is very reliable, level headed and hates drama (aka NOT the type of person to exaggerate stories). What is his wife like? What is their relationship like? How did they meet? Wife is very friendly. Also around 25 years old, level-headed, originally from Phoenix, went to school at the University of Minnesota (where she met Harry) and is now a full-time law student at Arizona State University. They got married right after graduating from college, so they've been married for almost

3 years.

Outside the distress of his case, which made him a bit eccentric, Harry was a charming young guy. He was also sharp-minded. He'd studied business at the University of Minnesota, all while balancing an active social life and extracurricular. That is also where he met his wife, Olivia. The two were a good balance – Harry was calm and level-headed, while Olivia was bright and bubbly, bringing out his goofy side that not many people were lucky enough to witness.

Olivia was originally from Phoenix, so when the two decided to settle down, they'd decided to do it close to her family. It would come in handy to have the grandparents nearby whenever they decided to have kids. In the meantime, Olivia was pursuing a law degree at the state university, while Harry spent his days at work.

Olivia describes her husband as a constant source of positivity in her life, with his ability to make light of any frustrating or stressful situation. But, unfortunately, he couldn't do the same with the incident that happened to him on a stormy night right here in the town they'd lived in all their lives.

As I continued perusing through the file in my hands, one sheet from the file stood out. It was the first email I'd received from Harry. He hadn't given me many details, specifying that he wanted to explain the case to me in person – because he was worried I'd turn him down right away. That piqued my interest, and I responded right away to set up a meeting.

Later that week, I met Harry in one of the local coffee shops in town. It was close to his high school, so he'd driven over right after the school day had ended. I'd grabbed a table in a quiet corner of the shop, toying with the warm cappuccino I'd ordered myself whilst waiting.

When meeting clients, I'd always try to choose a discrete, quiet spot to maintain some privacy.

I also made it a point to search up all my clients before getting involved with their cases. As I saw Harry walk through the door, I lowered my computer screen, which had all his social profiles and background checks pulled up.

We shook hands, Harry ordered tea for himself, and

we settled into our meeting.

"So, son, how can I help you out? And whatever we discuss stays between us from here on out."

"I appreciate that, sir. Especially because my case is a bit… unusual."

"Oh? I'm sure I can handle it. I've seen a lot in my day."

Harry began fidgeting his hands and shifting nervously.

"Yeah, everyone I've talked to about this has said that – and then they hear the story and think I'm crazy."

"I'll be the judge of that."

Harry went on to describe the incident that occurred some odd six months ago.

"Well, I was on a jog a few months ago. It'd been stormy, but it wasn't too bad, so I thought, why not? My wife, Olivia, told me to stay home that night. She was worried the storm would pick up all of a sudden. But I went anyway and told her I'd be quick. Boy, was I wrong."

Harry went on to tell me that that night, at 6:10 pm, he'd fallen on the sidewalk in 2021, and when he got up, he wasn't in 2021 anymore. He'd slipped back in time – to 1918. And when he returned back to the present at around 2:00 am, he woke up to see various firefighters and a police officer hovering over him, trying to get his attention. And when he'd tried to explain to them what just happened, they either just stared, unsure how to respond, or they just ignored him.

"Don't say I didn't warn ya," Harry said, with a weary smile on his face.

Of all the things I'd expected him to say, time travel certainly wasn't one of them. As Harry continued to relay the details of his night and as I began to stir up ideas in my head about how to approach this case, I was at a loss – for the first time in my career, I didn't know where I was going to start.

1918

The night of Harry's incident started like most other days in recent years.

That Thursday, he'd spent most of his day at the office trying to wrap up his work for the week and get ahead of the weekend. He was working as a junior executive at a local consulting firm, supporting local businesses in coming up with their business plans and keeping them afloat. He loved his work, not just because he could help people out but because he was in tune with communities around the city. Whenever he needed help with anything, there was always someone he could reach out to.

He finished the last of his reports and shot off a few emails before switching off his laptop and packing up his things. He waved to a few of his coworkers as he strolled down the hallway to the elevators, heading down to the building's parking lot. He jingled his keys in his hands and let out a big sigh, thankful that the week was coming to an end.

On the way home, he'd stopped at the grocery store to pick up some ingredients for dinner. He wandered through the aisles, tossing items in his cart as he saw them and hoping they'd come together to make an appetizing dinner. But as he chatted on the phone with Olivia about what else he needed to get, waltzing through the aisles aimlessly, he suddenly had a craving as he stood in the frozen foods section looking down at the frozen pizzas.

After proposing an alternative idea, they'd both agreed that they were too tired to cook an elaborate meal. So instead, they decided they'd get a large pizza from their favorite local pizza joint. He promptly left his almost empty cart on one side and strolled out back to his car, heading out of the parking lot and straight to NYPD Pizza.

About a half-hour later, Harry pulled up into the driveway of his home. Most nights, he'd pause in the driveway for a few minutes, just admiring their home and hoping to catch a glance of Olivia through the window that looked into their newly renovated kitchen.

They'd been living in this house for about two years now, but it only took them a few weeks to make it feel like home after they first moved in. They searched for some time when they were ready to settle down, but nothing seemed to fit into their vision initially. Finally, after months of back and forth with the realtor, they ended up visiting this house on a whim after seeing an ad in the newspaper. They describe it as love at first sight, that the house just 'spoke to them.'

The humble two-story townhome was located in a lively suburb of Gilbert. Many of their neighbors were also young working people around their age. Some of them had already started their families, as Harry and Olivia were eventually planning to do. A great school was just 15 minutes away, and a community park and recreation center were just a few blocks down. And if they needed access to the city, the commute was less than an hour, even with traffic.

With a simple silhouette and a palette of light auburn, the house fits right into the neighborhood while also standing out with its mix of Victorian and contemporary design. The wraparound porch was the envy of everyone who visited and one of the few reasons that the couple was almost immediately sold on the property. They'd envisioned their parents spending time on the porch watching over their future grandkids. The windows all around the house stood tall and wide, letting in rays of natural light during the day and giving the place its strong personality.

The interior of their house had been all Olivia's doing, for Harry had no creative eye whatsoever. They joked that hopefully, their kids would get Harry's brain, but not his sense of style.

Most of the furniture pieces they had were procured from their local thrift shop. Olivia preferred the antique feel over anything too modern; she felt that it would take away from the homey aura. But they were sure to throw in their 21st-century gadgets, including the flat-screen TV mounted on their living room wall, which was a necessity for nights on which Harry would have his friends over to watch the latest hockey match.

Then there was Olivia's pride and joy – their brand-new kitchen. While she wanted to keep their furniture older, she certainly did not compromise on the appliances that she'd be using to cook up a storm in the coming years. Fresh wooden countertops and cabinets complemented the stainless steel appliances. The paint was a deep sage, bringing a pop of color to their otherwise simple home.

The kitchen was their favorite place to have dinner. They'd made a pact to eat together as much as possible, without the presence of Netflix or the news. Evenings were the only time they'd get together during the week between Olivia's schooling and Harry's work, that they'd make a point to catch up and have some quality one-on-one time.

With the NYPD Pizza box spread open over the wooden island, they discussed the events of their respective days. Olivia had made progress with one of her professors in churning out some extra credit assignments for a better grade. Harry had finally had a meeting with his superior to discuss a potential promotion that was long overdue. All in all, they were both heading for success.

Harry's nightly routine was incomplete without his 2 mile runs around the neighborhood. Between his work hours and quality time with his wife and friends, he didn't manage to make it to the gym very often. And even so, he preferred a good run through the outdoors to any treadmill. The evenings were a much-needed relief from Arizona's intense daytime heat from the sun, so it was a perfect time to get in a workout without too much of a struggle.

This night, however, the weather was not as pleasant and peaceful as it usually was. Instead, there had been forecasts of an intense storm making its way through the state, set to make its landing in Gilbert that very night. They'd been following the storm in the news throughout the week but hadn't given it much attention until tonight.

As Harry and Olivia polished off the last slices of their meal, the trees outside their windows began to rustle harder as the wind picked up its pace. In the distance, they could hear the roar of the thunder as the storm approached. Though, to Harry, it still seemed far enough away not to be of concern.

Olivia, on the other hand, had been persistent that Harry should skip his evening run that day. She said it was totally unnecessary for him to be running out and about in a storm and that she didn't want to be alone in case the power went out. They'd found themselves in that exact scenario last year when a similar storm had visited their town. Harry had run out on an errand to find a particular tool that he needed to build their new nightstand. Olivia had insisted that it wasn't urgent, but once Harry started something, he couldn't bear to leave it until it was done. So he made his way to the hardware shop, not long after which there was a power outage at their home. Harry came back to a frantic Olivia running around the house looking for flashlights and told Harry he'd better not leave her alone like that ever again.

Harry, however, was adamant about keeping to his routine tonight. He joked that he especially couldn't skip his run today after having scarfed down over half of the large pizza. "I can't justify all that food if I don't run it off, darling!" he'd said.

So despite his wife's protests, donned in his favorite activewear, Harry headed out for his routine run. The last thing he'd heard before closing the front door behind him was Olivia telling him to be back before it was completely dark.

The sharp wind hit Harry like a punch in the chest as he made his way onto the sidewalk and graduated from a walk into a jog. A slight feeling of doubt came over him for just a second, but now that he'd left, there was no turning back. Surely he wasn't going to admit to his wife that maybe she was right.

On most nights, he'd pass by other avid runners in the neighborhood who had a similar routine to his. Sometimes they'd even band together and run the same route. Tonight though, as expected, the streets were empty, and Harry felt a sense of eeriness take over him. He didn't particularly like the feeling of being alone with the gusts of the storm.

He was just about to cut his run short and make his way back home when without warning, his sneaker got caught in a crack on the sidewalk, and he felt himself tumbling downward toward the concrete. As he fell, his vision blurred for just a second before he caught himself, managing to keep his head from hitting the ground.

Harry took a breath, gathering himself from a moment before pushing himself back upright. But as he did so, something felt wrong.

The concrete beneath him was no longer concrete. The harsh winds and sharp sounds of thunder had disappeared, replaced with a silence that he was sure he'd rarely experienced before in his whole life. And when his vision stabilized, he still couldn't see, not because of his eyes, but because it was pitch dark all around him.

As he kept waiting for the familiar scene of his suburban neighborhood to reappear before his eyes, Harry tried to keep the impending panic that was beginning to bubble up in his mind and his chest. He began to convince himself that he must have actually hit his head when he fell and that he was just having an incredibly realistic dream as he lay on the side of the street.

Harry didn't even realize that he'd been taking in deep breaths in an attempt to keep himself calm. Still trying to convince himself that he was dreaming, he thought he'd let himself explore his surrounding, hoping that maybe if he wandered around for long enough, he'd eventually wake up.

He got back onto his feet, brushed the dust off his clothes, and began to look for anything that was remotely familiar or for any sign of activity nearby. Unfortunately, the deafening silence was not giving him any confidence.

After a few minutes of hard blinking and turns in multiple directions, Harry decided it was time for him to move from the spot he'd been stuck to since he'd landed in this alternate reality that he still wasn't all too sure was truly real. He was afraid to move, worried that he'd find himself in yet another unfamiliar location. But standing around wasn't doing him any good either.

He picked a direction based on his instinct and began walking in a straight line, or what he'd hoped was a straight line. He couldn't be sure, considering all he could see ahead of him was darkness. As he walked, he began to count his steps in an attempt to distract himself. Eventually, the counting turned into him humming his favorite song.

As he was making his way into the third repeat of the song, he spotted it. A grey-toned light in the distance, barely visible from where he stood. If you weren't looking as hard and as desperately as Harry was, you might've missed it.

He was beginning to feel the weight of exhaustion, emotional and physical, settle into his eyes and onto his feet. But he was determined to figure out where he was, and right now, that light was the only lead he had.

His mind had been in and out of focus, so much so that he wasn't sure how far he'd walked by the time he began to make out some silhouettes where the light was shining from. By then, he must have walked at least a few miles, and he felt like his feet were ready to give out beneath him. But as the silhouettes began to turn into tangible shapes of small buildings, he had a spurt of energy from the hope of finding some answers.

The Coyote

Harry was an athletic guy. Aside from his daily runs, you'd often find him at the recreation center in his neighborhood, shooting hoops in the basketball court with friends from work, or doing laps in the swimming pool. He had tried almost every common sport in town and thought of himself as quite capable of getting through any activity with ease.

But as he sat on the barren ground in the middle of nowhere, still far from the light he was trying to reach, he didn't feel so strong. He just felt tired.

He'd taken a break from his walk. With no food and no water, he wasn't sure how long he would be able to sustain himself. He wanted to reach his destination – still unsure of what exactly it was – as quick as possible, but he was burnt out from the confusion and the walking so much so that he'd needed to pause for a moment.

As he sat, he thought he'd heard some rustling, but

he'd just assumed his exhausted conscience was playing tricks on him. He didn't have the energy to think about anything but get answers. He needed to figure out what was going on. He was sure he hadn't been gone for a long time, but he missed his home and his wife and just wanted to return to normalcy.

Taking a few breaths, he pushed himself off the ground with his hands and stood upright. He stretched a little, making sure his body hadn't gone stiff. After he felt a little more loosened up, he retied the laces of his sneakers, wiped the sweat off his forehead, and continued with his escapade.

Suddenly, Harry noticed movement out of the corner of his eye. Not having seen any sign of life other than himself for the past few hours, he started to feel the pressure build in his chest, and worrisome thoughts entered his mind. He still couldn't figure out exactly where he was, and with nothing to defend himself and no idea where he was, he was exposed to anything this world would try to throw at him.

He stopped his movements, hoping that maybe if he remained quiet, whatever it was lurking in the shadows would leave him alone. He steadied his breath, despite being exhausted from his trek through the empty, dry lands. It was taking all his focus to match the environment's eerie silence.

He turned his head from side to side, his concern elevating when he couldn't spot where the movement was coming from. Every time he'd look in one direction, it seemed like he'd hear something from the opposite.

After a few minutes of nothing, he decided to continue on his journey in search of civilization when he saw it.

Lurking in the shadows, he saw the outlines of an animal. As it moved closer to him, he began to make out the details; fur, a long, slow wagging tail, and pointed ears facing upward. Harry's eyes adjusted further, and the colors began to reveal themselves. The animal had an ashy brown coat, short but fluffed. Its shades lightened toward its legs, one of which stood out from the rest with a white paw. Harry's gaze shifted back up to the animal's face, and he was shaken by its sharp, bright yellow eyes - before him stood a magnificent coyote.

The two remained locked in a stare as Harry figured

out what his next move would be. He didn't know much about coyotes, but they were a common sight all around Arizona, so most people were familiar with the idea of them. They say that you must never run from coyotes because they are likely to chase you and feel the urge to attack. Rather, you must remain calm, and if a coyote tries to approach you, you should wave your arms, yell aloud, and make as much of a fuss as possible until it gets disgruntled and makes its own exit.

Starting to feel his legs fall numb, Harry shifted slightly, causing the ground beneath him to crumble under his shoe, which seemed to frighten the coyote as it made a slight jump at the sound of the gravel. It released a low whimper, moving a few steps further back. Harry wondered if he'd entered onto the animal's turf and it was feeling threatened.

In that moment, Harry wasn't sure what to do. From what he'd learned all his life, coyotes were scared of human beings. But he'd never faced one himself, so how could he be sure? His night had already been crazy enough; this was the last thing he'd anticipated.

So, instead of waiting, he decided to be proactive and fend off the animal sooner rather than later.

Moving at a snail's pace, he began to bend his knees, moving into a squatting position. The coyote watched him carefully as if it was ready to pounce at any unwarranted activity. Maintaining eye contact, he reached down to touch the rough gravel as he moved his hand around in search of a bigger rock, something at least the size of his palm.

Unsuccessful, he shifted slightly and slowly, not wanting to aggravate the animal looming in his direction. He placed his other hand down, moving it a few inches from side to side until he felt his knuckle touch something – a rock – a hefty one too.

Feeling somewhat emboldened, like he'd found a glorious weapon, he enclosed the rock into his hand and began to straighten his legs, moving back into a standing position. He clenched his hand tightly, afraid that the one thing that made him feel safe at that moment would somehow disappear and leave him defenseless once again.

The coyote had not moved from its spot; its eyes still zeroed in on Harry's form. He stared back at it, wondering for a second if what he was about to do would lead him to a worse situation than he was already in. But at that point, he really didn't have much to lose.

Harry inhaled deeply, took a fighting stance, stretched his arm back behind his head, and flung the rock as hard as he could in the coyote's direction. It didn't make direct contact but hit the ground right in front of where it stood with force and sent a spray of dirt in the animal's direction.

Harry waited for retaliation, but it didn't come. The coyote had stumbled back a few steps but remained calm, taking slow steps, not toward but around Harry.

He should've been relieved, but now Harry was visibly annoyed. If it wasn't here to attack him, then why the heck was it here?

"What do you want from me, huh?!" He was slowly losing patience. He was already frustrated being stuck in this ghost land that he couldn't interpret, and now this creepy coyote just had to show up.

He grabbed another rock from the ground, this time

a much smaller one, and tossed it toward the coyote once more. It barely even flinched this time.

He didn't want to waste more time trying to figure the coyote out and decided to start back on his journey toward the light. He needed to find another person and figure out what alternate universe he'd found himself in. So he began walking, keeping his eye on the coyote. It watched him, moving alongside him as he walked.

Because of the lack of light pollution, Harry swore he could see every single star in the sky. It was a moment of awe in a most troubling experience. And it was by reading the stars that Harry decided to make his way West. He could tell the direction. As a young kid, he was in the Boy Scouts for many years. Some of his favorite memories were from those years. He absolutely loved the experience – the training, his friends, his mentors, all of it. He couldn't wait to have a boy of his own join the Scouts and revel in all the glory as he did. Everything he'd learned, he'd committed to memory. Clearly, he'd made the right call because it was the only guidance he had right now.

The walk was monotonous, so much so that Harry

got lost in his own thoughts and didn't even realize that his new companion had disappeared. Suddenly he now felt even more alone than he did before the animal came along. Despite his initial irritation, it was comforting to see another form of life. It gave him hope.

After looking around and making no sighting, he trudged onward toward his destination. Alone with his thoughts, he began to think back to the circumstances that got him here.

He went through his entire day, looking for any signs that something was amiss. Everything was normal from what he could recall – like any other day, he went to work, went to the store, and then came home to his loving wife for dinner time.

Harry still wasn't convinced that this wasn't just a vivid dream. But as he grew more tired, and after his almost altercation with the coyote earlier, he was beginning to think that he may not be dreaming after all. The weather was humid and warm, and the terrain on which he was walking was a tint of red. It sure looked like Arizona. Could he really have been in the same place but woken up somewhere else?

And if that was the case, where the heck was he?

As he thought about his fall – how his foot got caught and how he managed to catch his head before it hit the concrete – another memory came to his mind.

Last winter, he and Olivia had decided to take a mini-vacation. Harry was set to travel for work to Tuscon for two weeks, so he thought, why not bring his wife along for the trip. She could use a break too, and she'd always wanted to visit the University of Arizona campus where her grandfather attended college many years ago. A smile came over Harry's face as he recalled all the times her grandfather would tell them to "bear down" when things got tough. Olivia missed him dearly, so the least Harry could do was help her visit his old stomping grounds.

They'd spent about a week or so there, and on one of their first days, they'd decided to take a hike on the nearby trail. They'd come prepared with all their winter gear, including Harry's cherished winter boots. He'd search high and low for the perfect pair; if anyone asked about them, they wouldn't be able to shut him up.

So the pair got dressed and headed off on their hike.

They were both fairly athletic individuals, so even a somewhat challenging hike wasn't a problem for them. They started off slow, picking up the pace as they made their way through the various inclines and uncleared spots that were covered with snow.

About an hour into their adventure, the trail became quite steep, and the path became more unpredictable. They slowed, still wanting to continue, stubborn as ever. Harry was in front, Olivia following behind him when he took a wrong step over loose rock and tripped over his feet straight into the snow. It was deep, enough that his impact wasn't severe, but not enough to keep his hands from getting a little scraped up when he tried to break his fall.

Generally a very steady and sporty person, Harry was always thrown off whenever something like this happened. He was a little embarrassed to have fallen in front of his wife, though, of course, she didn't pay heed as she went to help him up with only words of encouragement. After getting his bearings, they continued on with no further hiccups, making it to the end of the trail at the top of a hill overlooking the mountainous scenery. It was certainly worth the fall.

Harry was snapped back into the present, once again, to the sound of movement. This time it didn't take him long to figure out what it was. His friend had reappeared.

"Back again, huh? Don't you have something better to do? I thought you only chased roadrunners?"

The coyote only stared back, more silent than before. Harry continued to walk toward what he hoped was some form of life and that he was still in Arizona, and his companion followed along.

The Stranger

Harry could now feel every crevice and rocky texture of the barren ground beneath his feet. It was as if the soles of his favorite running sneakers had begun to deteriorate. But he knew it was the weight of his body that had been pressing down on them for the seemingly endless hours that he'd been walking toward the city.

His newfound friend had left him some time ago. After a few hysterical interactions and one-sided arguments, the coyote had not made a reappearance. Maybe it'd gotten bored of Harry. Or perhaps it was just a creation of Harry's exhausted mind, he wondered. Just like he wondered if this entire scenario was just a dream in his unconscious state.

The joints in his legs were aching, his mouth was parched, his lips were crusty, and his vision was going in and out of focus. He missed his wife, his house, his pizza. Several times on his journey, he'd thought about just laying down and going to sleep, thinking maybe he'd wake up back in the spot where he'd tripped earlier. He'd stand up, brush himself off, finish his run, and head on home before the storm hit. But he was determined to continue because, with a few more steps, he was about the reach the city that'd been in his line of sight for the last few miles.

The sun had set some time ago, but the only bright light had been his guide through the darkness, and as he came closer to the city, the minimal brightness from a few shops and street lights illuminated the rest of the landscape of old Gilbert, Arizona.

As Harry entered the town, he leaned over on the side of a building, catching his breath as relief filled his chest and air-filled his lungs properly for the first time since this whole debacle began. His ears perked up, and his eyes regained focus as he heard the chatter of people and footsteps. He made his way around the corner of the building and was met with the sight of people – real people!

Since it seemed to be quite late, it wasn't crowded, but there were still some folks muddling around, seemingly out for late-night strolls or running forgotten errands. But something wasn't right. The town only seemed to be made up of a few buildings as he could see from where he was standing the beginning of barren land once again just down the street. As he looked around, he began to recognize the street. It looked like the old Gilbert he'd seen in pictures. But... it couldn't be. He looked for the familiar water tower – crisp white with the town's name plastered in large dark font – the famous Arizona landmark that he drove past every day on his way to work. Where was the rest of the city? Where was the Gilbert he lived in?

Harry took a deep breath and stepped further into the town. Now that he'd come out of the shadows, and because there wasn't a crowd for him to blend into – not that that would've helped him anyway – suddenly, people weren't just going about their business anymore. Now, they were staring directly at Harry. Double takes, eyes widened, brows furrowed, and hushed whispers, all directed at him. They seemed to be looking him up and down, at which point he returned the favor, and his confusion turned even deeper. What were they all wearing? It was mostly men wandering around, but rather than the usual t-shirts and jeans Harry was accustomed to, they were tattered overalls and worn-out white button-downs. And a lot of them wore top hats. But it seemed that Harry was the one who was out of place, as they were staring him down in his polyester gear and uncovered legs.

He considered approaching someone to ask questions because now he had more than he did a few minutes ago. But every time he'd take even a few steps in a general direction, the people would disperse immediately.

This sure isn't going to work, he thought. So he continued making his way through the town, looking for anything that might be familiar or might explain where he was. Holding himself up every few steps against the side of the shops, he trudged along, avoiding other people as much as possible.

This street looks so familiar, Harry thought to himself. But at the same time, it wasn't familiar at all. He knew he'd never been to this exact location; the road wasn't even paved; it was just dirt, which he found extremely odd. As he walked past each storefront, he read their names. He came across 'Gilbert Bank' and 'Gilbert Garage.' There were a few men hanging out at the garage, looking him up and down as he walked by. He swore that this is where Joe's

BBQ was supposed to be, and boy did he wish it was because he was starving.

All of a sudden, Harry began to feel dizzy. The road and shops ahead of him began to look blurry as his vision faded in and out. He'd been sweating and dehydrated for hours, and now it was starting to catch up within. He needed to find some water, quick. But just as he was turning to continue his advancement through the town, he was met with an unpleasant surprise.

The heavy, wooden door of a shop swung open at that exact moment, knocking directly into Harry's already fragile figure, striking him right to the ground. He felt like this was the last punch – that he may not be able to stand up again.

He could feel like the ground under his back, the warmth of the stone seeping through his running gear into his skin. Unlike earlier, when he fell into this unknown scenario, he couldn't catch himself and most certainly felt a bump forming at the back of his head. All he could see above him was the dark sky, illuminated by mild street lights. He wasn't sure how much longer he could keep this up as his energy and his patience were dwindling.

As he was about to let the wooziness overcome him and fall into a slumber, through his blurry vision, he saw a figure standing over him. He first noticed his round face and dark hair brushed neatly backward. He had flushed cheeks, he was wiping sweat off his forehead, and his eyes were spread wide as if he'd seen a ghost. He was chattering over Harry's head and motioning with his hands, but he couldn't make out what the guy was saying.

The man disappeared, only to reappear moments later, now with an object in his hand, once again fluttering over Harry's exhausted body sprawled out on the sidewalk. Suddenly, Harry felt a few droplets land on his face, and he instantly came back into full consciousness.

"Water," Harry croaked.

He used his hands to push himself up, the stranger helping him by pulling on his shoulder. As soon as he was upright, he hastily grabbed the cup from the man's hand and threw the liquid back into this throat. He didn't even bother to check what it was but was relieved to find out it was indeed water. Harry downed the entire cup in a few gulps, like a starved fish who'd just been thrown back into the ocean. The water was warm but felt cool on his insides that had been melting in the humidity of the desert.

He was so entranced with hydration he almost forgot that there was a person crouched down next to him, still talking away. He hadn't heard a word he'd said this entire time.

"Thank you," Harry said, almost breathless. "Thank you so much, sir. You have no idea what I've just been through."

"Well, you are very welcome young man," he replied, the bewildered expression on his face not faltering. "Please, come inside. Let me get you some food. I am so very sorry for knocking you over like that."

Harry was now the one with the ever-confused expression. The way this man was speaking, it was so… formal. But he wasn't about to turn down a free meal. Distracted by his unquenched thirst and his constant state of confusion, he'd forgotten how hungry he was. But now, at the mention of it, his stomach began to clench and gurgle.

"Food… yes, please. I haven't eaten in hours."

With the kind stranger's help, Harry got back onto his feet. He was now able to get a proper look at the man who'd help him. Like his face, his body was quite round too. He was a hefty guy, donning a crisp white button-down and black slacks, with closed shoes. His hands were covered in white powder, as was some of his face. He must've been a baker. Harry looked up to see the door that had struck him and then at the storefront. 'Creed Grocery Store.'

Noticing Harry's curiosity, the stranger finally introduced himself as he guided Harry into his store.

"Raymond is the name. This is my shop, been here for years. And… yourself?"

"Harry," he replied, sticking his hand out for a shake, not really understanding the words he'd said, but enough to know he had introduced himself. Raymond hesitated but returned the gesture nonetheless.

The shop was rustic, nothing fancy. On either side were lines of shelves stocked with what he assumed were grocery items. Harry couldn't be sure because he didn't recognize any of them. Alongside the shelves were some wooden storage boxes, and on the right side were the counters and display cabinets which held various household items.

Raymond pulled out a stool for Harry and rushed off somewhere to the back of the shop. Harry took a seat, feeling like he was floating when he lifted his feet off the floor. He could feel the soreness and ache setting in and his pulse through his whole body.

Raymond returned speedily with a few slices of bread on a plate along with a glass of milk. Harry usually didn't like milk; he was traumatized by his parents forcing him to drink a glass each morning until he went off to college. But at that moment, it appeared more appetizing than anything he'd had before.

"Thank you, sir," he said quickly, unable to recall the kind man's name, as he took the plate and glass from his hands, not wasting another second before scarfing down the bread. He could tell it'd been baked that same day – it was nothing like the bagged bread he and Olivia kept in the fridge. They'd tried buying fresh bread so many times before, but it'd go bad before they got the chance to use it, so they'd given up that trial.

Once the plate was cleared of every last crumb, Harry took a moment, breathing in deeply, before going for the glass of milk. That, too, tasted different. Denser and creamy. The milk must've been fresh too.

Harry could feel the sugar in his bloodstream returning to normal. He was still exhausted, but his dizziness had faded, and he felt more perked up.

"Feelin' better, are we?" Raymond chuckled.

Harry gave a slight smirk. "I've had a hell of a day, sir. Actually, do you have a phone I could use? I'd like to call my wife."

"Sure thing, son."

Raymond hobbled over to the front of the shop, picking something up off of the table near the entrance before turning around and heading back over to Harry and placing the contraption down on the table in front of him.

Harry looked at the ancient phone sitting in front of him, equipped with a mouthpiece and a dial ring. He looked

71

back at Raymond, back at the phone, and then back at Raymond once more.

"Eh.. this is nice but, where's the real phone? You know, the cell phone?

"A what phone? I'm sorry, son, this is the only phone I've got. Not sure what you're referring to."

"Seriously? This is it?" Harry's frustrations are beginning to seep back in at this point, but he knows there's no use getting upset with Raymond. Clearly, he had no idea what was going on either, and he was just trying to help him out. So there, Harry was, trying to figure out if he could use this old gadget to contact Olivia. But even he knew that Olivia wasn't going to be at the other end of this phone line.

The Fall

It wasn't Raymond's childhood dream to own and manage a grocery store. In fact, most children don't say they want to own grocery stores when they grow up. They had other ideas – most people in Gilbert had dreams of moving out west in search of adventure and excitement rather than running a humble grocery store. When he was young, Raymond had similar ideas of what his future would be, but those weren't in his fate.

Raymond was raised in Pittsburg, where his father ran the town's most well-known grocery store for years while he supported the family. He put Raymond and his siblings through school. Their father was adamant that they all receive an adequate education, something he didn't have access to growing up. When they weren't in school, he encouraged them to stimulate their minds with reading, as well as with card games. Raymond's father was particularly fond of playing cards and taught all his children to play his favorite games. In the evening, after a long day of work, they would all sit together in the living room and play Solitaire for hours.

Growing up, Raymond, his younger brother, and younger sister would all spend hours in the store. Oftentimes they'd be up front, excitedly helping their father tend to customers. It was good for business – people loved interacting with the children. Raymond had memorized the layout of the shop; he knew where all items were supposed to be stocked, learned how to check inventory, and even helped his father with the accounts. Naturally, as he showed the most interest and understanding of the shop when his father retired, Raymond was expected to continue the family tradition.

As the eldest, he didn't have much room to argue or pursue another career. Someone had to take over the shop, and his father desperately wanted to keep the business in the family rather than sell it to someone else and lose their heritage.

When Raymond finally made his big move out west, he quickly became well-known to the community in Gilbert. Considering how small the town was, it was hard not to notice the brand new grocery store that had opened up along the main street. "Creed Grocery Store," he called it, after the store he'd spent most of childhood in. It quickly became the main source of the town's everyday needs.

As a child, Raymond was especially popular for his charm and kind demeanor. As an adult, he was known for that and more. He had continued his father's legacy keeping up the Creed's standard as the best grocer in town, this time in Gilbert instead of Pittsburg. If there was something you couldn't find in the whole town, Raymond was the man you'd go to, and he'd find a way to procure it for you. He found joy in helping others, and looking back; he wouldn't have wanted any other career.

Days in Gilbert were pleasant but uneventful, which is exactly how the town's people preferred it. They didn't like surprises.

The day Harry collapsed outside Raymond's store was like any other. Raymond had arrived at the shops early, done his morning inventory, and opened up the doors for the early shoppers of the day. All his customers were familiar faces with familiar shopping habits, but he was always around to help with anything new.

Once the morning rush had receded, Raymond often stepped out of the shop and had a chat with other vendors nearby. The store owners had all bonded over their journey and struggles from moving out west and became fast friends and supporters of one another. They all trusted one another not to steal or try anything funny, considering that if they did, it certainly wouldn't be difficult to catch the culprit. It could only be one of a few hundred people.

Raymond was in the midst of a conversation with the owner of the barber shop next door when he noticed someone keeling over right outside his store front. Without any second thoughts, he rushed over to help them. It wasn't until he was standing over the man that Raymond realized he'd never seen this person before in his life, and certainly not in his town.

Harry's dress was the most peculiar thing about him. Raymond was uncomfortable at the sight of his knees and had never seen this kind of clothing. The shiny material and style puzzled him. Who was this person?

Despite his concern and reservations at the sight of

this conspicuous stranger, Raymond would never turn someone away when they're in need of help. And Harry was clearly in bad shape. His dark clothes had gathered layers of dust over them, indicating that he'd been walking through the open desert. His skin was frighteningly pale, and he was in sweats, clearly dehydrated and feeling the warm weather. His eyes were completely dazed, and the poor guy couldn't even form coherent sentences. All he managed to choke out after a minute or so was "water."

After bringing him a glass and then helping him into the store, Raymond felt bad for the confused fellow who now sat by his stocked grocery shelves. He brought him some bread and milk; his father had always kept some in the back for the kids, and Raymond had picked up the same habit. It certainly came in handy at times like this.

As he watched Harry scarf down the food in what could've been a single bite, his nerves started to worsen. At that moment, he just wanted to help the poor man who had been lying on the side of the street. But now that he was inside his shop, he realized that he really knew nothing about this man; he could be anyone. And as Harry became more confused and agitated at the sight of the old phone that Raymond had handed him at his request, Raymond's anxieties only grew.

"So uh… tell me, son, where is it that you're coming from?" Raymond decided he'd better start asking questions. The sooner he could figure out who Harry was, the sooner he could decide what his course of action would be.

Harry hesitated before answering. He knew the correct answer – he was from Gilbert. But not this, Gilbert. By this point, Harry understood that he had to be in another time. But he couldn't wrap his mind around how that was possible. He was still convinced that there was a chance this was all a dream.

Nevertheless, Harry didn't want to create a commotion by saying something that would surely make him look like a looney. So he decided to go with a half-truth.

"Well, sir, I uh… I'm from Gilbert. But I was born and raised in Minnesota. I suppose you could say I'm uh… somewhat new here," he said with a low chuckle.

Harry's attempt to maintain a clear story wasn't

exactly working out, and he could tell by the look on Raymond's face. His eyebrows had turned inward slightly, and his slight smile faltered.

"Minnesota, you say? Quite the temperature change... But, son, this is a small town. Everyone knows everyone. Yet, I've never seen you. How long have you been in town?"

Harry stumbled once again. To this, he had no idea what to say. He knew this town was small and intimate; hell, you could see the entire town in one glance. There was no way he'd be able to convince Raymond that he'd been living in this same town for years. And there was also no chance that he'd insinuate that he was from a different time period altogether.

"Oh... actually, sir, I travel quite a bit, you see. Visiting my family back in Minnesota and all that. So I've been around for uh... a few years, but I don't socialize much."

Raymond most certainly did not believe that story. There was no way anyone came through this town unnoticed, let alone lived here without their name making its way through the rumor mill.

Harry's scene out on the street and Raymond going over to help him had already caught the attention of a few town's people, who were now lurking outside the Creed's windows trying to conspicuously eavesdrop on the pair's conversation. This hadn't escaped Raymond's notice, but he preferred to have some sort of an audience nearby in case anything went wrong.

As Raymond questioned Harry further – asking him what did he for work, about his family, why he moved to Gilbert – Harry's agitation grew. Raymond was convinced that he was crazy, but he would never say so, at least not to Harry directly.

In the midst of their conversation, one of Raymond's oldest friends, Jonathan, who ran the garage nearby, decided to involve himself in the situation. Being a close-knit community, everyone looked out for each other, especially those they've known for a long time.

Jonathan was one of the onlookers, and once he saw that the conversation seemed to be getting a bit intense, he decided he should step in. So he pushed open the doors of the grocer, the bells chiming as he entered, making his presence known to Raymond and Harry.

The two abruptly stopped their conversation as Jonathan approached them. Great, Harry thought to himself. The last thing he needed was another person showing his concerns and asking him the same questions Raymond had been asking for the last half hour that he was desperately trying to avoid.

"Hello, gentleman." Jonathan gave Raymond a pat on the back, letting Harry know that they were more than just acquaintances. It was almost as if his backup had arrived, and Harry couldn't help but feel a bit threatened.

Jonathan held his hand out toward Harry for a handshake. "The name's Jonathan. What's your name, son? I saw you fall earlier. Hope you're feelin' a bit better now."

Harry shook the man's hand, but he didn't believe he was genuinely concerned for his well-being. Surely, he was just looking out for his pal Raymond and wanted to get rid of Harry as soon as possible. But Harry wasn't about to make another scene; he didn't want to involve any more people in the situation than there already were. He just wanted to quietly figure out what the hell was going on.

"Pleasure to meet you, sir. My name's Harry. I was just telling Raymond here; I'm from Minnesota, but... I've lived in Gilbert for some time... I just travel a lot, so I haven't integrated into the community..." Having to explain himself again, knowing he probably wasn't making much sense, was causing him to stumble over his words even more. He was trying his best to sound sure of himself, but it was hard when that was the farthest from how he really felt.

Unsurprisingly, Jonathan had the same reaction to Harry's unlikely story – furrowed brows and a confused expression. But before Jonathan could question him any further, Harry decided to ask the questions for a change. Maybe he could get some information out of these two that could help him figure out where he was.

"Well, that's enough about me. I haven't learned a single thing about you both," Harry laughed nervously, hoping to get them off his back for at least a moment.

Harry shot back with similar questions that Raymond had asked him earlier. He'd asked if they were from Gilbert, how long they'd been running their shops, about their families. They responded, albeit with reservation and with short, stern answers. Clearly, they didn't want to give away too much personal information to a strangely dressed man they'd just met. So Harry switched up his queries and started asking more about the town. He asked about the population, about the different shops. Then, he asked something that perhaps he shouldn't have because it made Raymond and Jonathan's calm demeanors return to suspicious and confused.

"So, where's the water tower? I couldn't see it from the street," Harry asked.

"Water tower? There's no water tower in this town, son. Where have you seen one?" Raymond asked him.

Harry felt a pang in his chest; he couldn't tell if it was relief or anxiety. His pang turned into dread when he realized that somehow, outside of the realm of reality that he could comprehend, he was currently in the early 1900s Gilbert. And this was starting to feel less like a dream and more like a nightmare.

Back..

If you've never felt the symptoms of a fight or flight response, you should consider yourself lucky. Having your body react in a way that's completely out of your control and makes you feel like you're about to explode is no fun.

The more Harry conversed with the local townsmen, the more confused they all became. And with every answer that didn't align with what Harry knew about the Gilbert he was familiar with, his panic grew slightly deeper. Not only was he in the wrong place without any clue as to how to get home, but now he'd set off the two old men standing in front of him who were on the verge of turning the conversation into a full-blown interrogation.

Jonathan had been especially interested in figuring out Harry's story. He'd been shooting question after question at him for the last fifteen minutes or so – about his family, his upbringing, his education, his wife. Harry tried to dodge them or make up information that sounded believable, but the further Jonathan pushed, the less he found himself able to feign the truth.

In the midst of the questioning, Harry began to plot his way out of Creed's Grocery in search of help. He couldn't stay in this shop anymore. He could tell that Raymond and his buddy were suspicious, and things couldn't possibly end well for a strange outsider in a small town like this.

Harry diverted his gaze from the old townsmen standing beside him to the main street through the windows of the shop. He began to search for anything that could be a distraction or help get him out of this situation. He tuned out the chatter and zeroed in on a figure that looked like he could be the sheriff.

"Hey, buddy. Can you hear me?" Harry snapped back into focus at the sound of Raymond's elevated voice.

"Uh… yea, I heard you alright. Hey, would y'all excuse me for a moment? I just need to step out for some air," Harry said. Jonathan and Raymond looked at each other, seeming unsure for a moment, but of course, they couldn't stop him. He hadn't technically done anything wrong.

"Sure, son. Go ahead. We'll be here."

Harry wasted no time in pushing his way through the

front door of the shop. It was heavy, heavier than any door he'd ever pushed before. "Damn old infrastructure," he thought to himself.

He paused right in front of the store for a moment. In the frenzy of almost fainting, he didn't get a chance to look at the place – but that was the last thing on his mind. After waiting till Jonathan and Raymond became engrossed in their own conversation – no doubt about the strange man they'd just met - Harry refocused his line of sight on the sheriff he'd seen earlier and made a beeline for him.

Harry could feel the energy in his feet picking up as he sped to the other side of the street in his conspicuous running shoes. He might not have realized it, but tension and stress had been building up inside him since he landed in the desert, lost and confused. Now that he was fed and hydrated, the stress was becoming more palpable, and he wasn't sure how much longer he could keep himself together. He needed to get out of here, fast.

Just as he was about to reach the sheriff, who was now looking at him oddly, he had a moment of déjà vu. He took a step, and as his foot got caught in the unpaved road,

ZONA INVESTIGATIONS: THE 918 FILES

he slightly tripped. The sheriff called out, "Watch your step, son."

But, before harry could pay attention to the sheriff, he tripped again on his foot, causing him to slip in front of the local auto shop, and fall toward the ground.

Harry's eyes fluttered shut as he braced himself for the ground. He expected his hands to meet gravel as they touched the ground below him, but instead, they were met with a smooth, paved road.

At first, he laid still for a moment, keeping his eyes closed as he tuned into his other senses. He was trying to catch the familiar sounds he'd last heard outside the auto shop. The smells around him had changed. Instead of the dusty, barren scent of the desert, he was met with the scent of hot blacktop and gas.

He listened closely for the chattering of the people he'd been walking toward. But instead, he was met with a different voice – that of a woman. And seemingly no ordinary woman, because she surely did not speak in a familiar way. Her pronunciations were sharper, more direct – she was British.

She turned him on his back, and Harry opened his eyes and saw her looking at him, saying, "Hey, mister, wake up, please. Why are you lying on the road? Are you hurt?"

Harry thought he was back, but the tone of the woman stirred him, and he asked the lady, groggily, "Please tell me, I'm not in England. I don't prefer English tea."

The lady looked at him and lightly hit him across his cheeks, "Mister, what are you blabbering? Oh, God! I don't want another accident on my record. I am not that careless. What are you doing on the road?"

He was smiling but stayed quiet, looking at the sky. The lady was looking around and waving frantically to someone at a distance. Then, finally, she looked back at Harry and said, "Can you get up, please?"

Harry heard some footsteps and a gruff voice, "Yes, ma'am, how can we help you?"

The lady answered them, "Look at this man, he is laying on the road, and I cannot seem to get him up."

The officer faced loomed in front of Harry and asked him, "Did you meet an accident? Was this lady involved?"

The lady was frantic. She looked at the officers and said, "Officer, you have got to believe me. The bloke came out of nowhere! I was taking my usual route home because at this time there's no traffic – and usually no pedestrians! But I swear, I'm quite the diligent driver. So he just caught me off guard!"

The heat of the pavement was searing through his athletic shirt. He looked around to understand where he was. He was still lying down for some reason. He looked left and right and saw that familiar modern-day architecture, one-story storefronts, and paved sidewalks were on either side of him. . A little further up ahead was another familiar sight – Joe's BBQ! Harry knew then that he was back in the right Gilbert – his Gilbert.

Harry's momentary excitement was cut short by something else that also caught his eye – the red and blue flashing lights of a police car.

Harry began to push himself off the ground, but before he could even stand up, he already had two officers standing over him. He could hear them speaking to him, but it took a minute for him to decipher what they were saying.

The officer who looked at his face before said on the radio, "We have a dazed man out here. Can you roll fire? We have an adult male just lying on the road. He is awake and responsive. But there is something off about him."

Upon the arrival of the firefighters, he could see them searching his body for injuries. First, they flashed lights into his eyes to check if he was responsive. Then they began asking questions.

"Sir, are you alright?"

"Can you hear us?"

"What's your name?"

"Are you from around here?"

Among the numerous voices, the British lady's voice stood out the most.

"Sir, are you hurt? I can't even begin to explain how sorry I am for almost running into you. I swear by the Queen, it was an accident! One moment you weren't there and the next moment you were! I know it sounds crazy, but I don't know what else to tell you!"

Harry was dazed before when he saw her, and he looked more closely now for the source of the panicked, crisp speaker. He landed on a small woman. She seemed middle-aged, with blonde hair. He couldn't tell the color of her eyes because it was dark, but they seemed to be a light green. She was a bit short and stumpy, dressed simply in a t-shirt and jeans.

As she continued to apologize profusely, Harry's eyes focused above her head and behind her. Near the sidewalk was a bright yellow taxi. It should have been parked parallel, but instead, it looked like it had swerved to a degree and stopped abruptly.

"You know, I've been driving that cab for years, and nothing like this has ever happened. I swear I'm a professional, and I would never hurt a fly!"

From her confession-like words, Harry pieced together that this British lady drove the cab, and it seemed as though she'd almost hit him but had swerved away just in time.

"Excuse me, ma'am, what is your name?" Harry asked her.

"Miriam, sir. And you?"

"Harry. Please, Miriam, you can stop apologizing. I think I'm alright. You seem to have stopped just in time."

"Oh my goodness. You have no idea how relieved I was when you began to get up. I was so worried something terrible had happened, and you practically came out of nowhere. Like one minute, it is an empty road, and another minute, you are there on the street lying face down."

Not particularly interested in continuing the conversation, Harry gave her a curt smile and turned to the surrounding officers. Miriam was led off by a policeman, most likely to give a statement. Harry's eyes followed them to the police van that was parked right beside the firetruck. Quite a party for just one guy, he thought to himself.

"Sir, can you please tell us where you've been? You're covered in scratches and scrapes."

"Uh…"

Another firefighter piped up. "You look like you've been through hell, dude. Can you tell us what happened?"

Harry wasn't sure that he was ready to get into what

he'd experienced just yet. He hadn't received a positive response from the old townsmen when he'd tried to explain where he was from, and so he expected a similar reaction from the folks hovering over him.

"Just bear with me but… what year is it?"

The firefighter who sat right next to him, checking his breathing, furrowed his brows. "Excuse me, sir?"

"Uh… what year is it? Just want to make sure I got my head on straight, haha…." Harry nervously tried to make the question less suspicious.

"Sir, it's 2021. What year do you think it is?"

Harry let out a sigh of relief that he didn't even realize he was holding in. "That was it. Just wanted to make sure my head was on straight, you know."

The firefighters were definitely not convinced and began to check again for any signs of neurological damage. They asked him to say his ABCs and count backward from 100. They asked him his name, age, occupation, all the standard stuff. Like,

"What is the month?"

"Tell us who is the president right now?"

"What state do you live in?"

He answered everything right, but he kept looking around the street, taking in the modernity, glad to be back in the right time zone.

This didn't go unnoticed by the officers or the firefighters – Harry was sure he'd heard one of them say to the other, "This guy seems a little 918." He wasn't sure what they meant, but it definitely didn't sound good.

Once they were done with their inspections, the firefighters helped Harry up from the ground, led him over to a bench, and gave him some water.

While drinking water, he caught sight of the water tower and chuckled, "Can you believe there was no water tower back then and here in this moment, it is standing as a grandeur masterpiece."

The firefighters looked at him and then at each other. They seem confused at his excitement to see the water tower that has been there for years now.

While Harry sat on the bench, once again feeling

dazed and confused, a policeman walked over to take a statement from him regarding the events of the night. They'd taken his name and personal details from him earlier to run it through the system and figure out who he was.

"Alright, Harry, can you start by telling us the last thing you remember?"

Harry still had no intentions of telling the truth about his adventures, so he pretended like he'd lost time.

"Officer, I left my house around maybe 7 pm like I do every evening. My days aren't complete without my evening runs. And well, the last thing I remember is being about 20 minutes into my route when the storm seemed to pick up. And after that, it's totally blank until I woke up right here."

The officers looked at him and looked unconvinced of his story. Harry sensed it and asked, "Am I in trouble?"

There was a pause for a minute which looked like years had passed.

"Alright... Well, Harry, we looked up your information. You're a long way from home, and around 10 pm, your wife reported that you're missing. In fact, dispatch told me that officers were at your house earlier tonight responding to her report. It's now 2 am, so that's quite some time that you can't account for. Any idea where you got those scratches on your knees?"

Harry looked down at his legs – the firefighter from earlier was right; he was in bad shape.

"No idea, sir. I assume I must've fallen at some point, and it happened then?"

"Harry, you've gotta give us some answers here. We can't figure out what happened to you unless you work with us."

Harry began to get nervous again, as he had in Raymond's grocery store. Eventually, he'd have to tell someone what happened. And hey, maybe they'll believe him in the present.

"Well, officer... I've been here but... not here..."

The officer's expression remained unchanged. He clearly wasn't impressed with Harry's answer, to no fault of his own.

"I'm sorry, I'm afraid I don't understand."

Harry began to get frustrated, running his hands through his hair, having to refrain from pulling at it.

"I can't explain it, but... I was in Gilbert. Just... a different Gilbert."

"A different Gilbert? I wasn't aware there was more than one," the officer replied, his voice dripping with sarcasm. Harry sighed to himself. Of course, they didn't believe him. Who would?

The officer looked over to the firefighters. No doubt they'd exchanged notes about Harry's odd statements and demeanor before speaking with him directly. They must've gotten a kick out of having to deal with yet another crazy guy.

"Alright, well, we're gonna call your wife and let her know you're okay. Stay put, though. We're not finished here just yet."

With that, the officer walked back to his car, leaving Harry alone with his thoughts once again.

Cheater

A few hours ago..

"Come home before dark, will you?" Olivia shouted as Harry went out all geared up for his evening run. She shook her head in denial, knowing that Harry would do what he wanted to. No storm could stop him from his run. Olivia thought to herself.

She got herself busy in the kitchen, doing last-minute scrubbing for an early night. Harry would not be back for an hour, and the storm looked closer than ever, evident by the constant sounds of thunder. She tried not to worry about Harry, but it was becoming a constant nag.

After an hour, the wind had gained momentum, and the tree outside was swaying. But, unfortunately, Harry had still not returned. Olivia was now worried. Thankfully, there was no power outage this time. Oddly, he did not return after an hour. Maybe, he stayed somewhere till the storm passed. The wind is quite fierce. Olivia thought to herself.

After another hour, the storm passed away, and still, there was no sign of Harry. She called some of his friends and inquired about him, but no one had any clue. Olivia was panicking now, and her mind was racing. Every worst-case scenario came to her mind. What if something had happened to Harry.

"I would just wait for a few more minutes and then report about him. What if he is really lost out there? Or did something happen?" Olivia said it out loud, pacing the living room.

After a while and a few more calls to his friends, Olivia was sure something had happened. It had been three hours and Harry's evening runs were always thirty minutes to an hour-long. She called 911 and reported her suspicion that her husband was missing.

After two hours, at exactly 11 PM, two police officers were outside their house, asking about Harry and his appearance. Olivia told them everything, and they left, saying, "He will be back. The dispatchers will alert all the patrols out right now, so they will be on the lookout. We will call you once there is any news."

Olivia shut the door behind them and was now waiting for their call. Finally, at exactly 2 AM, the phone rang and informed her that the police had found Harry lying on the road. She noted the address and drove toward the location – half-fussed and half-relieved, wishing Harry would be safe.

***

Harry was told that his wife would be arriving any moment and he felt relieved as he was sure that Olivia was the only person who would believe what happened.

He tried to make sense of everything that had happened in the last few hours.

He went out of the house for a run, and due to the storm, he thought of cutting it short. So he turned, slipped, and found himself back in the early 1900s. It was Gilbert surely, but not this modern 2021 version. He talked to the resident of that small town, and again, as he approached the sheriff, he slipped and found himself back in his Gilbert.

Even his own mind knew the story was bizarre, and people would have a hard time believing it.

After a few minutes, he saw his wife's car approaching the place. She looked disturbed as she got out of the car. An officer approached her. After confirmation, he led her toward where Harry was sitting.

The officer was filling her in with the details, "... called you as soon as we found him. A cab driver found him lying on the road."

"Excuse me, did you say lying on the road?" My wife interrupted as she frowned at the officer.

"Yes, Ma'am. It's bizarre. Neither the cab driver made sense that he appeared out of nowhere, nor did Harry let anything sensible out. Of course, we called you as soon as we ensured that his vitals were okay. He doesn't seem to be making any sense, though. I asked him where he had been, and he just seemed confused and said I was here, but not here."

"I don't understand, but thank you, officer. I would look into this. Am I allowed to take him home?"

"Yes. I just don't know which other Gilbert he talked about."

The officer led Harry's wife to him and went away toward his car, making final notes on his notepad.

Olivia looked at the disheveled Harry and hugged him, "I am glad they found you. What have you done to yourself? I told you not to go out in the storm."

Harry hugged her back and said, "Am I glad to see you. You have no idea where I have been. I know, I should have listened to you. But, well, I am here and alright, so let's head home."

"At least tell me what happened and where were you for this long? And what does that officer mean by lying on the road and a different Gilbert?"

"Ah, of course. Let's go home."

Harry did not want to tell everything there. Instead, he wanted to go home and take a long hot shower. And then sit down and talk about everything with Olivia. She looked confused and could not understand where Harry was coming from.

They had a silent journey back home, for Harry was thinking about the best way to describe the absurdity that happened.

Harry went into the kitchen, took a bottle of Powerade, and chugged it down upon entering their house. Olivia looked scared as she saw Harry and the state he was in.

"Will you tell me now what happened?" Olivia said in a small voice.

Harry looked at her, set the bottle down on the counter, wiped his mouth by the back of the hand. He looked intently at Olivia. It was difficult for him to decide where to start.

He went into the living room and sat on the sofa. Olivia came and sat next to him and put a hand on his shoulder, and said, "Harry, you are scaring me now."

"Do you think time travel is possible, Olivia?" Harry asked her cautiously.

"Yes, that sci-fi nonsense you see in the movies."

"Well, what if it happened in real life?"

"What? You must be joking if you said that could

really happen."

"No. I am not. Because I think I just traveled back and forth in time."

Long pause met Harry's words. Olivia was looking at him without any expressions, and it seemed like he had told her a peculiar joke.

"Okay, did I miss the punch line here?" Olivia looked skeptical.

"No, I am telling you the truth. I went out running, the winds were getting fierce, so I turned but accidentally slipped. And I did not faint or anything. Instead of hitting the road, I landed on the ground, but it was the desert. Like out in the middle of nowhere desert, and it was really dark. I first thought that maybe I hit my head pretty hard, but I was sure I had saved my head from the fall. I could see the light very far in one direction, so I walked toward where the light was coming from. Maybe it would answer the confusion as to where I was. I don't know how many hours I walked, and the entire time, a coyote kept following me. And then I reached a small town. There were a few people here and there, and the infrastructure was old. Even the people were not wearing modern-day clothing. I tried to ask someone, but I'd approach any of them. They would just disperse. They would just look at me really weirdly and walk away."

"I was not among them, and hours of walking had me dehydrated, so I collapsed in front of what I think was a Grocery Store, and a guy named Raymond helped me. He gave me water and food. Can you believe this, Olivia? He gave me fresh milk and bread. Anyways, they started asking me questions, and I wanted to call you. They gave me the phone with the dial and the earpiece. They did not know what cell phone even was. That was when I knew that I was not in my time. I had somehow gone back into the 1900s, and Gilbert was very tiny at that time. Just a handful of people, and they knew everyone there."

"I wanted to know more, so I looked around, and I guess I saw what I thought was the sheriff. I was about to make my way to him, slipped, and then found myself laying on my back getting yelled at by some British lady. I cannot believe what has happened. It is so bizarre but, all this actually happened."

Harry got up from the sofa and looked at Olivia for

the first time since he started his story. She was looking at him with wide eyes and an open mouth. Harry knew at that very moment that she had not believed a single word he said.

Olivia shook her head, held her palms out, and said calmly, "Okay, I like the story, but where were you really?"

Harry thought Olivia would believe him, but she thought he was joking with her.

"I know I joke a lot with you. But this is real. I was not here. I mean, I was here but not in the same period. There was no water tower, no paved roads, and no Joe's BBQ - nothing. And the men wore silly outfits."

"Come on, do you think I am that naïve? No water tower?"

"But, I told you the truth. I did tell you where I was."

Olivia could not believe what she was hearing, and Harry was trying desperately to make her understand. Finally, Olivia stood up, took him by his hand, and led him upstairs.

She went into the bathroom and turned the shower on. Then, she grabbed a fresh towel from the dryer, laid it next to the shower door, and looked at Henry in a get-in-the-shower type look.

"I don't need a shower right now. I want to know how it is possible," Harry said to her as she stood there looking at him.

"Dear, I am glad you are home, safe and sound. The winds did knock you out for good. But it is okay. Some Advil and a good night's sleep never fails. You take a shower, unwind and come to the room to get some sleep. Okay?"

"But…" Harry started to say something, but Olivia gave him a peck, told her everything would be alright, and she went into the room, leaving him no choice but to take a shower.

Harry could not understand how he could explain what happened to him was real. He knew that it was not a hallucination or a dream. Harry was sure that he would talk to Olivia again and explain the incident once more.

The following morning, Harry woke up to see Olivia's side of the bed empty. He could hear her in the kitchen. He dressed and came to the kitchen.

"Morning, you did not go to the office?" Harry greeted Olivia.

"Today is Saturday, Harry, and it is almost noon," Olivia said in a calm tone which Harry could not place right.

"Oh, so can you cook me our Saturday special?" Harry tried to lighten the atmosphere in the kitchen.

"I am already on it. The coffee is in the machine. Pour yourself some. I was bringing the tray to the bedroom."

"That is quite okay. Unfortunately, I could not sleep well last night."

"Yes, I am sure of it."

Olivia placed the plates and the skillet on the island and gave him a hearty portion. For a moment, they ate in silence, and then Harry said,

"I still do not believe what happened yesterday. It is so incredible to be true...."

"Because it is a lie," Olivia interrupted him.

"What?"

"Your story, Harry. I thought you hurt your head

pretty hard last night. I really thought that some Advil and a relaxing shower would sort everything."

"No, Olivia, I am telling you the truth."

"Please, do not think of me as insane. Either tell me the truth to where you were or simply don't lie. 1900s, Gilbert, Raymond, desert, coyotes. I mean, what!? I cannot think of any reason why you made this story...."

"Because it is the truth and not a made-up story. I was really in the old-time Gilbert. It was just an old-looking town like you see in the movies. Everyone knew everyone, and I stood out between them. I may have been dehydrated, but that wasn't till after I walked forever, and I know I didn't hit my head, and I, for certain, didn't have a concussion...."

"Okay, so hear this out, Harry. You went out for a run right before this storm, and you tripped yourself and ended up in 1900 something."

"I know it sounds weird, but that is what happened. Why won't you believe me?"

"Because that's ridiculous. Have you ever heard in real life, someone time travel?"

"No, but…"

"But, tell me what happened exactly. I don't want to hear about your dream."

"I told you, Olivia…."

"I don't want to hear that."

"But you will have to."

Things were getting heated up on the kitchen table as Olivia was not ready to listen to Harry, who was now getting frustrated as to why no one would believe him.

"Dreams are not that vivid, and I did not hit my head anywhere to have a concussion, Olivia."

"But hallucinations are that weird."

Harry was about to retort back in anger when Olivia held out one finger.

"I am not going to argue on this, whatever you saw. I just want to know where you were for eight hours if you did not faint."

Harry looked at her. He opened his mouth to speak but knew that Olivia was not going to listen to anything. So he left the kitchen and his half-finished plate on the table.

Olivia followed him, asking him where he went, and Harry kept saying, I told you the truth. They had another heated argument which ended up with Olivia calling him a madman and suggesting he consult a professional.

A couple of days passed, and it was getting unbearable for Harry to look past what had happened with him.

Was it really time travel or a horrible dream? Hallucination or concussion? *'Maybe I did hit my head,'* he thought.

Olivia was not listening to him, and he was not sure with whom he should discuss this incident. The officers and Olivia did not believe anything he told them. Would anyone else? There were so many unsolved questions in his mind, and he wanted the answers to each one of them.

He knew he was not mad, and it was insulting to ask to consult a therapist when he knew what had happened. He wanted someone to understand him and conclude what might be the reason for such an inexplicable incident.

It was an incredible but traumatic experience.

"It did look like a dream for a few moments. But everything was so realistic that... ugh. What is truth, and what is false? There's no way I just imagined a coyote following me. I cannot seem to think straight. Would anyone ever believe me, to what I witnessed?" Harry thought to himself.

He was sure to discuss it again with Olivia when she was back home.

Later in the evening, Harry was watching the television as Olivia came home from her work.

"Evening, dear," greeted Harry.

Olivia gave him a stiff nod and busied herself in taking off her coat and shoes. It was getting pointless as Olivia had not talked to him properly since the last argument.

"Will you cut it out?" Harry said as he switched off the television.

"I am sorry, cut what out?" Olivia replied without even looking at him.

"You know what I am talking about. You have been giving me the cold shoulder for days now."

"I have done nothing of that sort."

"Will you look at me and talk about what is going on?"

Olivia finally looked at Harry. She put her hands on her hips and demanded, "Why would I look at you? Since that dreaded day when I told you not to go out, you have been acting strange ever since. First, you do not tell me where you went, and then you mutter in the shadows. What do you want me to do?"

"I am trying to make sense of what happened, okay? I am not muttering to myself. I am trying to...."

"Oh, please. Not that again. I am sick of that story. So I went to the officers who found you on the road, asking them what exactly happened. They said some lady cab driver found you. She said it was like the street was empty one minute, and you appeared out of nowhere the next minute. Seriously, they were laughing as well. So they reckon you were running, and the storm took you off the route, and the cab driver may not have seen you and hit you when you came around the corner."

"What a nice story, and that is not made-up at all, right?"

"At least it has got some logic, Harry, unlike yours."

Harry's face was getting red. He was tired of explaining to Olivia.

"And how would you explain the dust and the scratches? Is the cab driver crazy as well? Do you think I ran that far? It's so far from here."

"It was a windy night, Harry, and you did say you tripped, so…."

"So, you are going to go with the logic here, Olivia."

"At least it makes some sense. Or my head is cooking something else too."

"And what it might be?"

"That you are cheating on me, and you probably paid that cab driver to help you come up with some absurd story to hide your real intentions."

Harry would have laughed at the statement if he was not irritated and shocked by the response. Olivia's face was flushed with emotion, and there was a moment of silence.

"That's what you think?" Harry asked Olivia calmly.

"Yes. I think you should take a break. Maybe go see a...."

"I am not mad, Olivia."

"Then, my dear, do not act like one. I am tired of you thinking about it. Even if it was true, think about it as a dream and move on. I am tired of us having this argument. I'll go and change, okay? And then we will have dinner together."

Olivia left Harry in deep thought if he indeed was a man without reason.

JASON CVANCARA

Madman

The morning was crisp and fresh, and the flowers were shining with dew in the sunlight. The light breeze was soothing, and the clouds were scattered all over the sky. It was indeed a picturesque moment that could make anyone feel refreshed for the day. But, not Harry.

It was almost a week since Harry's time slip, and since that day, he hardly had a good night's sleep. People were considering him a lunatic madman who was telling nothing but lies. Not even his wife trusted him.

All these people were right in their mind frame. Even if someone came to Harry to tell him that they time-slipped, he would never have believed them.

So, he stopped telling people about his little paranormal adventure and went to search online. On this particular Saturday morning, he sat with his laptop on the kitchen table with a cup of coffee.

He had been searching about timeslips for two days.

There was a lot of information about the topic, but nothing solid enough to explain what had really happened with Harry.

One of the articles described time slip as a fictional plot device that allows people to travel through time by unknown means. The traveler typically has no control and no understanding of the process, and it is mostly never explained. It happens independently, and there is no set duration to how much time they will remain in either the past or the present.

Harry was quite sure that the explanation best described what happened to him. The article further stated about a person named Frank who went out shopping back in 1996.

He wanted to buy a CD and was looking to visit the HMV store. However, as he walked near the Post Office, he felt as if he was engulfed by silence.

After a moment, he was paused to see a small box van similar to the ones in the 1950s speed across his path, narrowly missing him and honking its horn.

Then, Frank realized that he was standing in the middle of the road and was looking at Cripps to what should be Dillions. The book store was replaced by some ladies' store showcasing handbags and shoes.

Frank followed a young woman inside, and to his disbelief, the store's interior switched back to a bookstore. He asked the woman if she saw the same thing, and she replied, "Yes, I thought it was a ladies' store, but this is a bookstore. So I might have stepped into the wrong store."

After reading the article, Harry tried to search more about Frank, but he could not find any other information. However, it was solid evidence that others have also found themselves in somewhat similar situations.

He took a sip of coffee and further searched for anything that could make sense as to why he time-slipped. He landed on a website that had podcast on numerous subjects. Finally, he found the one that another article had hinted.

His wife entered at the same time he was going to listen to the podcast.

"What are you doing on the laptop at this hour?" asked Olivia.

"Nothing, dear. Just had to send an email," Harry replied calmly, minimizing the screen and closing the laptop.

"Oh, I thought you were still going on with that dream of yours. Please forget what happened. I saw the books that arrived yesterday. 'Time-Slip, Is It Real!?' 'Is Time Travel Real?' 'Time Travelling –the Real Story!' Are you for real?"

"Is it a problem if I am trying to find what happened to me that day?"

"Ugh, never mind. What do you want for breakfast?"

"The usual."

Harry and Olivia ate their breakfast in silence, and the weekend passed away without any further mention of the time-slip adventure.

It was becoming an obsession for Harry. After searching online and reading articles, and watching YouTube videos about time-traveling, he was sure that what he witnessed was not a dream.

If anyone just believed him, it would be easy for him to understand the superficial happening. But, no one was paying him any heed.

On his way to the office on Monday, he passed the same place where he had slipped back to the old Gilbert. He thought of reenacting the whole process again to see if he would time-slip again.

The whole day went by, distracted. Harry's work was not proper at all and, by midday, he was called by his manager to look at several corrections. The usual chatty Harry was not conversational at the workplace at all. The idea kept coming to his mind, and he just wanted the day to be over.

During the break, he sat at the table with his untouched sandwich, deep in his thoughts, when one of his colleagues, Ron, sat down in front of him.

"What is the matter, Harry?" Ron asked.

Harry looked at him and answered, "Nothing. Why do you ask?"

"You look worried. I can sense something is wrong."

Harry hesitated for a moment. No one understood anything before, so Ron would behave the same way.

"Have you ever had something weird happen to you?"

"Ya, a lot of times."

"Really, Like what?"

"Like the other day, I had this sense of Deja vu that I had been to that new restaurant before. It opened in east Mesa about two or three weeks ago, and I went there with my wife. But, I am sure I have been there before as well. Quite weird, right? Why do you ask, though?"

"It is nothing. Actually, nothing makes sense anymore…."

"Is everything alright at home?"

"Actually, my wife thinks I am a cheater."

"What? Why?"

"Where should I start? I went to a jog the night of that storm, and after thirty minutes, I cut my run short, and as I was turning back for home, I sli…." Harry looked at

Ron, who was listening intently. For a moment, Harry thought of telling everything but, he did not want to become a part of another "Harry is mad" conversation, "I fell down and had to hang out under this covered park area till the storm was over."

"And she must be thinking that you went off to some other lady or something."

"Yes, something like that. I don't know. I might be having some deja-vus too."

"Don't worry, deja-vu are common. They can happen to everyone everywhere. Now, the restaurant story might have to do something with my childhood. Maybe, I went to a Chinese restaurant when I was young. So, everything is linked to your memories, experience, and the subconscious."

"I am sure Old Gilbert was in my conscious," Harry muttered.

"Sorry, what old Gilbert?" Ron asked with a raised eyebrow.

"Nothing, for weeks now, I am thinking about how

this Gilbert would be?"

"Unmodernized and a few shops here and there. No sign. Just a handful of people who knew each and everything about everyone."

Harry was shocked to hear such an apt description.

"How do you know so much about Old Gilbert?" Harry asked.

"Oh, it's in the...."

"Ron, the drawings need a touch-up before we send it to a client, and Harry, the boss, is calling for you again," Cheryl interrupts the conversation.

"We are coming. The break is almost over as well," Ron called out to her and then said to Harry, "Do not worry and eat that sandwich. You look pale."

Harry tried to eat his sandwich. In fact, he nibbled it rather than ate it.

All day long, his head kept thinking of what would happen if he went and slipped again. Would he be able to pull it off again, and if it happens, would he be able to return?

All kinds of questions kept creeping into his mind, and as the day ended, he could not be much happier. Finally, he signed out of the office using a finger sensor and drove to where he had fallen.

He tried to slip but couldn't as it is difficult slipping when you do not intend to fall. Harry tried to jog and trip himself, and as he tripped, he attempted to drop the same way as well.

It was pretty tricky to reenact what happened on that stormy night.

After several failed tries, he was able to copy what had happened. He jogged from a distance and tripped himself at the exact moment and with the precise turn. He fell down on the road and closed his eyes.

When he opened them up, nothing had happened. There was no darkness or silence. It was the same place at the same time. So he tried it again, but nothing happened.

He tried to slip walking, thinking about all the articles he read and podcasts he listened to. All the notes he made of how various people traveled, but whatever method he used, he was not able to time-slip again.

One of the men in that neighborhood had been looking at Harry for quite a while. "What on earth is that guy doing? The people who move here keep getting weirder and weirder," he thought.

The man called Harry and said, "Hey brother, are you okay?"

"Yes, I am okay," Harry replied with a long face. He was dismissive about everything. He was really hoping it would work.

"Did you lose something?" That man asked again.

"Yes. Perspective" replied Harry, before going back to his car and driving away, fuming.

The man looked at Harry as if he had gone mad. Harry did not care about what the man thought about him. He was only interested in finding answers.

Harry knew that he was not senile, and it was definitely not a dream. But then, all of a sudden, all the articles seemed faked, that maybe people did that for becoming famous.

Back in the 1900s, when technology had not advanced, such stories like time-traveling or UFOs would seem bizarre and true. And all the gossips and conspiracy theories that followed would really contribute to the factor.

He was angry at himself and fate for putting him in such peril. He thought of doing some more research later that night.

After Harry finished his night-time routine, he took his laptop and started searching again. But, much to Harry's dismay, nothing new came on the web except the keyword "Unusual," which bought something up on his screen.

Off to the side of the screen was a google ad with the heading, "Involved in an unusual incident in Arizona." It was about a private investigator, Charles G. William, and his private detective agency, 'Zona Investigations." The tag line said, "Chuck will solve all your queries and investigate anything – even the unusual ones."

There was a number in that advertisement too, which Harry noted in the diary he was making his notes in.

Things were not looking good for Harry as with each

passing day, it was becoming a headache. What, how, and why did it happen. And why won't it happen again? Should he wait for the storm to come, or maybe it happened every year at the same time and the same place.

A few more weeks passed, and Olivia felt that Harry was destroying his mental health. Harry was doing everything as his regular routine but, there was something weird about him. He seemed lost, confused, and looked like he was always searching for something.

Harry just wanted answers, and he was getting none. On another Saturday, when Harry and Olivia were having their breakfast together, Olivia asked, "Harry, you should stop thinking about it."

He looked at her and resumed eating without saying anything. He had lost his patience with explaining that he was not stupid or a mad person.

"I am serious. Look at you, Harry. Since that day, you have done nothing but obsess about that dream of yours. Okay, if it was not a dream, I saw what you wrote in your notes, read that book you ordered, and even went through the podcasts you were listening to. Do you think you are suffering alone? Yes, it is hard to believe it, and that is what everyone went through who had such occurrences. I am really sorry; it is still hard to believe that you went back in time, but ....."

"But what, Olivia, did you not see the starches? Or how did they find me? Even that cab driver said I appeared out of nowhere. So how did I come up at that place when you know it was way out of my regular running route? So tell me, do you have answers for that? You know I will never cheat on you. Why even think like that? I could simply have said; I was at my friend's place, honey. Why would I do such an elaborative scheme and have officers and firefighters involved?

"Everyone thinks I am crazy or have gone completely off the hook. I am done explaining to everyone that what happened was real and not a dream. I thought, you will understand, but you accused me of something I never did. I didn't know where to go, who to talk to, so I started searching on my own to ensure that whatever happened had an explanation. I cannot live my whole life, Olivia, thinking that what I witnessed was a figment of my imagination. I cannot accept that end to this story."

Harry was breathing heavily by the end and had tears in his eyes. Olivia stood up, went over to him, and placed a hand on his shoulder.

"I am really sorry, Harry, for accusing you. I know you won't do anything like that. But you need to understand, dear, that this is not something that can be digested easily. No one will believe you, and even if you find those who you tracked down in that notebook, they will say the same thing that I am saying. I am so sorry that this happened to you. And I can understand that it is unsettling but, I will not allow you to lose yourself after something to which the answers do not exist. And lean on a story that no one believes," Olivia said, wiping his tears.

"There is one person who might believe in unusual things?"

"Who, that Chuck person?"

"How do you…wait, you read the notebook. Of course, you will know."

Harry stood up and rushed to his desk. Olivia

followed him.

"Harry, what happened?"

Harry said nothing and opened his laptop, and wrote Zona Investigations in the search bar. Within milliseconds, the screen came up with everything related to the agency.

Harry clicked on the second search link, which said, "CHUCK SOLVES THE UNUSAL MYSTERY."

The article was about how the person claimed to see the ghost of his mother. She asked him to give everything to his young step-brother and that she would want him to become a man of himself.

The man's wife then contacted Charles to look at this phenomenon. When he investigated, it was found that the man was being drugged by his step-brother. The medicine made him hallucinate, and then his brother would call him and ask him for the money and property.

The article ended with a note from Charles himself, "There are many things that people go through, and not everyone can understand them. But, there are answers to everything on the earth if you look closely. And if you cannot find answers, then some things are better left alone."

Harry looked at Olivia as they reached the end of the article.

"So, you are going to call him?" Olivia still seemed skeptical.

Harry did not respond, and Olivia left him alone in the room after a little pat on the back.

He went back to his research, and after a few more articles and podcasts, he was determined to ask for help. It had been more than a month now, and Olivia was right. He could not let this go on for long. Something was to be done, as Harry took out his cellphone, dialed Charles' number, and waited for him to pick up his phone.

Investigator

His foot was pattering against the wooden floor while his fingers were tapping in a rhythm on the long mahogany table. Charles was on the phone, listening intently to what was being said.

"I wish someday I could throw away this phone for a few minutes of bliss," Charles thought to himself.

"Let me see what I can do. I am already looking for clues...." Charles stopped talking as there was an interruption from the other side.

After a few seconds, Charles continued, "As I was saying, I am still digging, so do not worry, Mr.Grey. I assure you that the next time I call, there will be news. Now, if you may excuse me, I have another call coming in."

Charles bade goodbye and cut the call, sighing. He had only lied to Mr. Grey, for he did not know that his lie would become true the next second.

The phone vibrated on his desk, and for a moment,

he wished to ignore the buzzing noise. But, he, himself, had chosen this line of work that needed extra concentration and extreme and seemingly constant interactions with people.

Sighing loudly, he picked up the phone and looked at the ID. It was a local number. Charles swiped up the green call button and spoke into his cell, saying, "Zona Investigations, Charles G. William here. How can I be of service?"

There was silence as Charles listened intently to the call.

"Can you please confirm that you got my contact through a google ad?" Charles asked.

Charles nodded as he took out the file labeled 'New' and picked up a pencil.

"Let me note down what you are saying. Can I have your name?"

A pause and Charles wrote, 'Harry.'

"So, Mr. Harry, what is your story? Please describe it in detail."

As Harry told his story, Charles' brows furrowed. Charles never interrupted his clients, but he could not comprehend what he was hearing, so he had to intervene, "Excuse me, did I listen to you correctly? You went for a run right as a storm was coming in, and then you accidentally slipped to find yourself in the Gilbert, but it seemed like you were in the past. You interacted with people there and came back after slipping again on the road. The place was the same, but the time period was different. Thus, the surrounding was not the same. Is this what I heard, Mr.Harry?"

There was affirmation on the other side which was met by a long pause from the Charles. So long that Harry had to ask if the line was still connected.

"Yes, I am here. I am sorry, but I am afraid that we have to end the call here and give you an appointment so we can meet. I prefer that the person come to my office or meet somewhere for coffee and discuss in detail. It makes things easier to understand and evaluate."

Another pause, and Charles continued, "Of course, we can meet in the office as you prefer. Come on this

Saturday by 4 in the evening. We would have plenty of time to discuss. I believe you have my address. Perfect! Have a great day."

The call was very absurd as Charles was left in deep thoughts afterward. In so many years of his personal and professional life, he had heard about time-slips but never encountered someone who actually went through them. Yes, he did look into wildly unusual circumstances, but everything had a logical explanation to it.

His last case was at one of the older residences in downtown Phoenix, where the residents saw lights and heard whistles in their backyard. Mr. Peter and his family were adamant that some ghosts were trying to make them leave their house.

Though the story was oddly funny, as Charles had suspected, the densely packed trees in the backyard were making the whistling noise. And as for the lights, they were simply cars passing by on the road, and at times, their lights would reflect just right off the stop sign into their window.

The case got solved pretty quickly, and it got the hype as well because Mr. Peter was relatively well-known and very connected with local politics; in simpler words, he liked attention no matter the type. Some newspapers made fun of the whole incident, and one of the headlines stated, "If they cannot detect car lights, how will they notice the lighting problem increasing day by day."

Charles chuckled at his thought and looked at the time. It was getting late, and he stood up from his desk, stretched, and walked out to his car, thinking about dinner and Harry's bizarre story.

Saturday arrived quicker than Charles had anticipated. He straightened himself in his chair as he waited for Harry to arrive. He looked around his organized mess of a workplace and promptly gave up the idea of tidying up.

He knew things would become messy again, and it was too much to handle for him at the age of forty-seven. But, as long as he was able to find items in this chaotic mess, everything was fine.

Harry was on time, and Charles welcomed him in his office. Charles noticed that Harry was looking all around. The long brown wood-paneled walls were decorated with certificates and accolades from when Charles served in the

ZONA INVESTIGATIONS: THE 918 FILES

police and military.

He also noticed that Harry was keenly interested in the pieces he was either gifted by the clients or the ones he bought himself from various international visits he made when needed. Harry was looking from the paper piles on his desk to the file desk cabinet in the corner.

"Did you find the office with ease, Mr. Harry?" Charles asked Harry, who was still transfixed with the office's interior and Charles' collections.

"Oh... Yes, yes! The address was simple enough," Harry replied.

"Please have a seat then."

"Thank you."

Harry sat down in front of Charles as he took his seat behind the desk. At 5'6, Charles was on a perfect height to have a comfortable conversation with his clients. However, before Charles could say anything, he noticed Harry looking at one of the most peculiar things in his office.

Charles noticed how Harry looked with a creepy expression as the object he was viewing was quite weird but was his most prized possession.

"Ah, I see. You noticed the all-seeing eye. My spy, for all matter intact, knows if the person is lying or not."

It was a glass paperweight with an eye in the middle and an inscription in the end, "I came, I saw, I'm now creeped out," written in cursive writing.

When Harry did not comment anything about it, Charles continued, "This is a gift from my sister. Please relax."

Charles chuckled, sighed, and thought to himself, "This happens every time. They come with the most peculiar of stories, and looking at usual things creep them out. I guess only Heather can know the absurdity of things I go through every day. I really like my gift."

Harry gave a slight nod and looked at Charles, who understood that the fascination had gone and they could talk business again.

"Mostly, I meet my clients at a coffee shop of their choice as I love to step out of this office once in a while. But, since you insisted no audience, here we are," Charles said as if there were no interruptions.

"Oh, yes. I don't mind the audience, but my story is not... what should I say? Something that can be easily digested," Harry answered him.

"I can understand. People are not open to new and different."

"That is why I came to you, Mr. Charles. I saw your ad and read the article on your recent discovery about the winds. I do feel there would be a logical explanation. Unfortunately, though, I highly doubt it."

"Do not worry. I will be recording our interview as it allows me to concentrate on my client. So you won't have any problem with it, right?"

"No, not at all. Before I narrate what happened to me, let me ask you something."

"You will be needing a background, right?"

Harry nodded, and Charles sighed. It seemed that Harry felt awkward and needed some time to calm down before talking about the incident.

What Harry asked was not new to Charles as every client wanted to know about him. Charles gave his introduction for the ninth time, which he never minded because he was very proud of his law enforcement experience.

"I saw you were mesmerized by the awards, certificates, and the pictures, and you are right in assuming that I was a cop. After high school, I joined the Air Force and then got out. Then, I was hired by Phoenix PD. After working behind a desk for others, I opted to work behind a desk for myself. I started this investigation business, and since then, I have been helping people solve their cases that the police cannot handle...."

Harry interrupted him and asked, "How come the police cannot solve a case, they have more expertise than you?"

Charles smiled and answered, "I have been asked this question quite a few times as the cops should be able to solve everything. Of course, I might not have the exact answer as people are different, but there are rules that they need to follow rigidly. And let's say that a private investigator can bend a few of those rules. Do not get me wrong, I am a man of principle, but we do have some freedom remaining in the jurisdiction. Of course!"

Charles knew that Harry was anxious, and he wanted him to feel at home so everything could be discussed with ease.

"Would you like some coffee?" Charles asked.

"No. So, how many cases have you solved till now?" Harry abruptly inquired.

"Ah, Harry, to be honest, I really do not keep count. But, with the papers and files lying around, you may have some idea that I do not sit idle in my office. I have been working for 8 years as an investigator, and I have come across some pretty random ones."

Harry nodded again and looked at the one corner of the room.

"I was about to hang up when you were silent for so long after hearing the story over the phone. But, then you asked me to come here. So, can you solve this mystery?" Harry asked as if he was not sure why he was sitting in an investigator's office.

"Tell me from the start what happened?"

"I had pizza with my wife, and then, as usual, I went for a jog in the evening. But, the storm was approaching that night, so I wanted to cut the run short. And... as I took the turn... I slipped. And I found myself basically in the desert... It felt like that.... But then I started walking and eventually got to a small town. As I looked, it was Gilbert.... Not this one... old.... the dressing of people was different.... And no sign or anything, just a hand...."

"Wait, so when you slipped, did you hurt your head?"

"No, I did not. I caught myself before it hit the pavement. But my hands did not meet the street but something like rock and dirt."

"Are you absolutely sure?"

"Yes! Do not call me crazy. Everyone has been calling me that since they found out what happened."

"No, I am not calling you crazy. Calm down."

"Why should I? Everyone is calling me a lunatic, thinking I am making up stories of time travel. Why would I?"

"Calm down, Harry. No one here is calling you a lunatic."

"But, you do not believe me either."

Charles sighed, got up, and went to the far side of his office, where his coffee machine lay silently. He opened the hatch, chose the brew, and pressed start. Within seconds, the whole office was filled with the aroma of the coffee.

"I told you I do not need coffee," Harry said, sounding irritated.

"It is my special brew. A few years ago, I started a side business selling coffee and called it Zona Coffee. Figured I'd put my obsession to good use," Charles smiled.

"I actually bought a bag of that for my sister when she was here a few weeks ago. Small world."

"Well, tell her to buy more so I can retire. Ha!"

Harry laughed and nodded as he took the cup of

coffee Charles had offered. After that, there was complete silence in the office except for occasional sips as the hot coffee had made the environment warm enough to let Harry relax.

Charles knew how such clients were handled. He was very down-to-earth and friendly. However, Charles never liked talking about himself much, making him very cautious about what he shared with everyone.

He was interested in Harry's story, so he decided to open up a little bit, "You know I have researched on time travels and looked up about people who have been involved with time slips. There was this case in England, and I really did go to the place where it all happened, just to see it for myself. So, please do not think you will be judged here. I have had a fair amount of absurdness with many cases, and I always found a logical solution to every scenario."

Harry looked intently at him and took another sip. Then, finally, Harry sighed and told him what had happened that night. How he went for a run and slipped to find himself in a deserted plain and how a coyote seemed to track him from a distance until he reached the only source of light. He also told him about the appearance of the Gilbert he had found himself in and its people and the two gentlemen he met and conversed with.

Harry went into minute details about everything, from eating at the store to asking for a cell phone and identifying the sheriff.

"... and before I could talk to the sheriff, I slipped again and found myself surrounded by police officers and a cab lady who then called the fire department. They questioned me, and they thought I'd hit my head when I tried to tell them everything. But, of course, they were not the only ones. Everyone thought I had gone bonkers. I mean, one of the cops even used the radio code 918, which I later found out meant that the person was crazy. That I might be crazy.

I researched and looked up people who went through such scenarios. But, no one believed them, and they were not able to solve the mystery. So, I came to you as this incident is causing a strain on my physical, emotional and mental state."

Charles listened to everything in silence. He was sure there would be some explanation, even if we consider it a dream. But if it were a dream, he would have woken up at the same place. Was Harry sleepwalking? Charles knew that coming to conclusions so early would not be helpful.

"I see. Do not worry."

"How do you come in the picture now? Like what will you do to solve this?"

"Anything I could. First…."

Charles was about to explain when he made a mistake and looked at his phone. It was ringing, and he had silenced it for the meeting.

"Sorry, just give me a moment."

Harry nodded as Charles took the call. He talked to someone up in Payson for two minutes who wanted help trying to figure out what was happening to his cattle. He then took his phone and put it upside down, and continued to Harry, "My phone rings all day, and you won't see me sitting idle at all. It drives my wife crazy."

Harry laughed, and he felt relaxed. There was something about Charles that made him satisfied that his case would be solved.

Charles continued, "So, I was saying that I would be talking to everyone and would be looking at all the details. Do not worry."

"Will you be able to help? I mean, is there a way to somehow show I'm not losing my mind?"

"I will give it to you straight. But, unfortunately, your situation is very unusual, and I cannot be sure before studying intensely about each and everything. Of course, there is a fifty-fifty chance, but I am sure there would be some logic behind this. As I told you before, I did look into time slips and travels but, this is my first time investigating it."

"I do hope that you come up with something because it is driving me crazy."

"Well, let me start some digging, and then we will hold another meeting. Okay?"

"Of course."

Charles stood up and held his hand out for Harry. They shook hands, and Harry thanked him for his help. Then, before Harry left the office, he turned around and said,

"I almost forgot, how much would you charge?"

Charles laughed loudly and answered, "This is precisely why I often get in trouble with my wife because I over-deliver, and I hardly ask for that kind of money. Anyways, do not worry. We will discuss that later. Right now, you go and take some rest."

"It is hard to believe that you accepted the story so calmly. But, I am assured that something will come out of this, thank you."

Charles smiled at Harry as he left the office. Charles sighed deeply and started the coffee machine before returning to his desk. It was already six in the evening, and there were still a few cases to summarize before moving toward the new one.

He looked at his phone and saw that there were messages and miscalls from various clients. There were numerous emails to answer as well.

Charles closed his eyes for a moment as the coffee maker pinged to signal that the coffee was brewed. Then, he got up, took his coffee mug, and looked outside the small window in his office.

The murky grey sky did not help, so Charles returned to his desk, set the cup aside, opened the mail to answer as the phone started ringing again.

"Ah, and my life goes on. But, this time-travel case is going to be an interesting one," he said to himself as he swiped up to answer the call and settled back comfortably.

No Proof

"I hardly see you anymore, Charles. Where have you been, and what are you up to these days?"

Charles was sitting with his friend Bryan at the Bosa Donuts. They were meeting after a long time, discussing life over a cup of coffee. As he took a generous sip of the brown liquid, Bryan asked Charles.

"Ah, it is just the tedious work, Bryan, that keeps me hinged."

Bryan looked at a small handkerchief lying in front of him and smiled, "Our work here is all about details, see the dotted imprints on this napkin is not just dots, but actually, BD punched into it."

"What does a donut shop napkin has to do with what we do?"

"Charles, Charles, Charles. I have told you so many times. The tiniest details that set the truth and false aside. Remember the Flitwick case we worked on together?"

"That case was complex. A murder happened on the porch with the family inside the house. There were no witnesses to what had happened, but you pinpointed the details."

"Yes, I never saw such a case in my 40 years of experience, with apparent answers but no evidence to charge against the murderer. The police department does have a few setbacks; otherwise, we can crack the case."

"Yes, Bryan! You have a keen eye, and you inspired me to become an investigator when you opened your own private firm."

"Ha, I am an inspiration. I knew not!" Bryan laughed out loud, "Hey, 918?"

"918! The 918 file is getting bigger and bigger, and hard-to-believe cases keep coming in. The one I just got contacted for is the most bizarre."

"What is it about? I thought you liked the unusual cases?"

"Yes, I did. But, this one is odd," said Charles looking distraught.

Charles did not know where to start. So, he simply stared at his coffee as he thought about where to begin.

He felt like Harry as if people wouldn't believe him if he even narrated the story. Charles looked at Bryan and was comforted, knowing that being an investigator and a magnet for the crazy himself, he would understand the realities of the case.

After another hour of coffee, talks, and narrating Harry's story about time travel, Charles waved goodbye to Bryan and headed to the police station.

"Mr. G. Willam, what brings you here? It is so good to see you. How have you been?"

Sergeant Joel Kaminsky came greeting Charles as he entered the station.

"Joel, how are you? I heard you got promoted?"

"Yes, sir. I cannot believe it. Guess if you stick around long enough, they'll promote you out of pity. Ha!"

"You were perfect; you deserve it."

"Thank you, sir. Please tell me how I can be of help

today," asked Joel.

"I sent in a request online for a report involving one of my clients. Not sure if you remember, but it's the one who they found on the street allegedly hit by the cab?"

"Okay, sir, have a seat, and I will look to see if it's ready."

After getting all the information, Joel hurried down the hall and returned with the paperwork in his hand, and handed it to Charles. He then started flipping through the pages looking at the details. It was very brief and had just a few points.

"Joel, is this all they have on the case?"

"There was no case, sir. The cab lady denied that she hit the guy and said things that did not make any sense. And we reviewed it when you called one of the officers who were present there."

"And? Did you find anything unusual?"

"Sir, the only thing unusual was Harry's attitude and this disheveled state we found him in."

"There was a storm that night. What if he was caught in the tree or something? It says in the report here, 'We found the man... a cab lady called... information... disheveled state... making no sense of words... his story did not resonate...'"

"Yes, sir. Harry did say he'd been to the past. Prolly hit the concrete too hard. A little 918 if you ask me."

"Maybe," Charles mumbled. He then thanked Joel and turned to leave.

"Chuck, not to tell you what to do, but if I were you, I'd probably contact the British lady who drove the cab. She had called the day after asking if the guy in the road was ok and seemed pretty centered. Maybe meet her for some tea and crumpets or whatever it is that the Brits eat."

"That's the plan, Joel. Well, maybe not the crumpets part."

Charles walked to his car, unlocked the door, and sat on the driver's seat. He did not start the vehicle, though. He closed his eyes for a moment, leaning his head on the headrest.

Charles was sure that there was something more to the case that did not make it into the report the police department had. Everything up till now was summed up with the story that Harry told him, but there was no explanation for the time slip.

He never made assumptions this early in the case, but Charles thought for a moment that maybe Joel was indeed right about Harry hitting the concrete. But then he remembered the talk he had with Harry's wife the following day Harry made the visit to his office.

"Can I speak to Olivia?" Charles deiced to call her.

"Yes, this is Olivia. Who is this?"

"I am Charles, from the Zona Investigations. Your husband Harry came to me regarding the investigation of the peculiar situation he found himself in on the night of the storm."

"Oh, so he did contact you?"

"Yes. Can you kindly tell me what happened exactly?"

"Well, that day started off as it always does. We went

to the office, came back home, and had dinner. He went out for a run even when I told him that there was a storm. When he was not back at his usual time, I got worried and called all his friends. None of them came back with a positive reply, so I put in the missing person report. After a few hours, around 2 am, I got a call that Harry was alive and was found on the street."

"When exactly did he leave home?"

"Exact 7."

"Has anything like that happened before? Or is there anything else like a medical condition or something? Does Harry have epilepsy or dementia?"

"No, no! He is not crazy."

"Ma'am, please do not get me wrong. I am merely asking this, so things get clear to me."

"It is okay, and yes, this has happened for the first time. I have never seen him this tense. First, I also thought Harry was going bonkers, but then I realized he was telling the truth or maybe half-truth. Something happened that night, and I also want to know the answer."

Back in the car, as Charles recalled the conversation with Olivia, he was sure that they were really an average family, and nothing extraordinary ever happened to them up till that day.

Charles started his car and went back to his office to look for loopholes and brainstorm. Finally, he reached his office and sat behind his desk, putting his head on the table. He tried to calculate and make sense of all the information he had till now.

After a while, he sat up straight, took a notepad, and wrote,

Visit the street,

Look for the cab driver,

Have a conversation with the historians,

Visit the old Gilbert library,

Visit the Gilbert museum.

He jotted down the basics to find the most answers as the only solution that came to him was comparing the old Gilbert with the version that Harry had narrated.

His first visit was to the old museum with relics, historical documents, and pictures of the Old Gilbert. He was getting frustrated as the more he looked into the details about Old Gilbert, the more truth could be seen in what Harry told Charles.

As he collected evidence to support his theory, he stepped out of the museum and checked his phone. It was from an unknown number. He was not answering random calls, or any calls in that matter, as he was spending his resources to investigate the time-slip case.

Reluctantly though, he picked up the call and said, "Charles here."

A crisp male voice answered, "Mr. Charles, we are calling from the Gilbert Grab A Taxi service. We received your call about the information on a cab driver, Miriam. Is that right?"

"Yes, she was involved in an incident with Gilbert PD around a month ago in the downtown area? I need to speak to her."

"Sir, we are a little confused. There is no such cab

driver who was involved in an incident."

"But I have a police report right in front of me saying Miriam, who works for your company, contacted an individual lying in the roadway."

"Miriam, do you know her last name?"

"No, I am afraid not. It was written in the records but must have slipped my mind. I do know she is British?"

"Ah, that Miriam. I know exactly who you're talking about. Let me connect the call to her."

After a moment of silence, a polite British accent greeted the call. Charles greeted back and went straight into business, but she cut him down and asked him to meet her at Starbucks tomorrow at 4.

Charles hated Starbucks but felt that this was the only chance for him to have another White Chocolate Mocha; he was never going to that place on his own otherwise.

Everything was aligning but, the most intriguing part was how the description of the Old Gilbert matched with that of Harry's. It did not resemble but was an exact match to what Harry had told Charles.

He thought of calling it a day but wanted to take a look at the library as well, as all the articles were archived there, and he was sure that if something happened, there would be a ripple effect.

Someone might have reported an incident where they found an eccentric, strange man roaming the streets of Gilbert. Charles knew that his search of articles would include the years 1900 to 1920.

He went to the library and asked for the archived newspapers and articles. He was led to a room dedicated to Gilbert's history and was happy that he could do his research in peace.

He started looking up the historical evidence of when the town was built and how it has progressed over the years.

He was happy to find a computer with access to the library's database, which allowed him to search deep into history. It would have taken more time to search it manually, but the information was not valuable.

He already knew that the town was small, and with a handful of people living at that time, everyone knew each other. This led Charles to the idea that if a man wearing modern clothes materialized out of thin air, it would become a piece of news for centuries to talk about.

But, there was nothing in the online archived articles and papers, so Charles searched the library manually. After an hour, he concluded that this could not be done in a day, and he would be back the next day. So, he wrote the file number and went home to note down what he had found.

The following day, Charles came early to Starbucks and ordered himself the White Chocolate Mocha he loved. While waiting for Miriam, he realized that he did not bring the recorder. It was supposed to be an official meeting, and it was intriguing that he forgot such an important thing.

Harry's case was not as simple as it seemed, and the more resemblance he found, the more enthralling it became for Charles to contemplate everything. He wished that Miriam would just come and say that Harry was jogging and she hit him by mistake.

An older lady came in and introduced herself as Miriam. She looked British in every way. Charles stood up, motioned her to sit down after a brief greeting, and went straight to business, asking her to narrate the whole story.

Miriam was a chatty person, and she gave in more details than just the night of the incident after ordering herself the same White Chocolate Mocha Charles loved. However, Charles was inwardly happy about not bringing his recorder, for the battery would have died down before getting to the main point.

After another bout of who she was as a person, Miriam came to the point, "So, after a long day of driving, I was driving down Gilbert Rd, after waiting at Starbucks as the storm passed. The road was quiet, and I was humming my way... believe me, the speed was slow. I think it's only about 25mph down there. As I was about to take a turn, a man came out of nowhere. No one was even on the sidewalks, but it was almost like he materialized out of thin air. He hit the road face down before I halted to a screech. A second late, and I would have run over him."

"So, there were no other pedestrians on the street at that time?"

"No, not as far as the eyes could see, and I have perfect eyesight. But, as I said, there weren't even any on the sidewalks. There was no one down there, which was odd in its self."

"Okay, so what happened next?"

"Well, he was on the street, face down, and I panicked. First, I thought to just drive around him since I figured he may have just been drunk, but my conscience got the better of me. Plus, they also have cameras."

"Cameras?"

"Yes, I think they have traffic cameras."

Charles's eyes sparked up that he might have a piece of evidence now to what actually happened. However, he did not comprehend the information as his mind was racing already. Miriam went on to tell him about the cops arriving and how they questioned them. Charles was forced to listen again when she said, ".... he materialized out of nowhere."

"Are you really sure about it?"

"Absolutely. No one believes that I am saying what I saw. For a few days, I was really disturbed by how he may have come out of nowhere. I guess some things cannot be explained."

Charles knew she was right, and now he had another task added to the list. First, he had to contact Gilbert Police to see if they had cameras in that area.

"Thank you, Miss, for your valuable time. But, unfortunately, I must leave now. I have a few things to do before the day ends."

"Of course, Charles. Have a great day."

"Same to you."

Charles gave her a nod and headed out of Starbucks.

As he was driving home, his phone rang, and the caller's id showed Harry's name. Charles picked up the phone and put it on speaker.

"Hey, Charles. How are you?" Harry said in a small voice.

"Harry! I am good, what about you?"

"I am okay. Thank you so much for asking?"

"How is the investigation going?"

"It is going well."

"What have you found? Found the answer yet?"

"Harry, this stuff requires extensive exhaustive research and patience. However, I am doing everything I can to help you."

"Yes, I know. But.."

"Let's meet in a week. Okay?"

"Perfect."

The call ended, and Charles went about exploring every inch of this case. First, he found out that there were no cameras in that area, and three more trips to the library archive section showed him something that made him pause....there was indeed no water tower in the Old Gilbert.

Charles now had enough information to declare the story as truth, but there was no significant evidence if Harry had really time slipped.

Whatever the case was, Charles knew that he had been to the Old Gilbert for no one would know what people wore and that there were only a handful of people residing in the town at the time.

165

Charles wanted logical reasoning as to what happened and why. He was not the type who just relied on instinct.

As he waited for Harry to arrive after the week of intense searches and mind-blowing revelations, he was sure that there was still something missing. Unfortunately, he knew that he might never find a solid answer, but he was sure to find a logical explanation.

Harry came into the office and shook hands with Charles, who motioned him to have a seat.

"Before we start, Harry, I forgot a crucial point in the pieces of information you have provided. What was the color of the Water Tower in the Gilbert you supposedly visited?"

Harry looked at Charles and made a face as if he did not quite understand the question, "What do you mean by color, Charles. I remember telling you and everyone else that there was no Water Tower."

With wide eyes, Charles knew at that point, unless Harry was indeed 918 and had done a ton of research, Harry was not lying about anything. He did not make the story up, and everything directed that he indeed time-traveled somehow. This case was becoming more and more interesting, but Charles was not about to close the case file shut without any solid evidence.

Enough

Thrashing around in his sleep, Harry woke up with a jolt. For a moment, he thought he had time slipped into another era yet again until he realized he was only dreaming. For weeks, he could not sleep well, and if he could, the dreams would make it harder to stay asleep.

He picked up his cellphone and looked at the time. The screen showed that it was Saturday, 5 AM. He found the information so frustrating that he cursed loudly. Olivia stirred a little in her sleep but did not wake up.

Harry sighed and got out of his bed, and went to his study to distract himself. However, he knew that nothing could be done about his case as there was no solid evidence. Charles told Harry everything he had found in his investigation in their last meeting.

His dream felt so real, like the time he actually slipped the time, and for a moment, it made Harry realize that maybe it had been a dream all along.

Harry might have simply slipped, hit his head on the road, suffered a concussion, and had an illusion that he went back years. After thinking for a while, he opened his laptop and decided to write an email.

"Dear Charles,

Please accept my heart-filled gratitude for investigating my case. I was sure there was some explanation for the whole situation. I wanted to tell everyone that I was not crazy, but I guess I had a hallucination that was too real. I might have been walking through Gilbert thinking it was the old one.

I think we should leave the further investigation. Meanwhile, I will try and forget what happened to me.

Thank you so much for all your help,

Regards,

Harry."

He reread the mail and was just about to send it when the study door opened, and his wife, Olivia, peeked from behind.

"What are you doing here, love?" she asked him bleary-eyed.

"Nothing," Harry closed his laptop without sending the email he had written for Charles.

"I know it's nothing. Why are you up at this time?" she asked.

"I had a dream. I could not sleep afterward."

"Yes, it is going to be on your mind if you keep reading these books and keep looking for a reason."

"What can I do then?"

"Take the books and throw them in the trash. Then, delete the browser history and stop searching for such articles. Think of it as a dream and move on from it."

"Olivia, it is not that easy to think of it as a dream. Even Charles thinks I am telling the truth."

"Where is the evidence, Harry?" asked Olivia with annoyance.

"That is what Charles and I are looking for. I don't want anyone to call me crazy anymore."

"I know. That is why I am saying, leave this behind and move on. People will soon forget everything, and no one will talk about you anymore."

"I will become the dark humor at parties, like that poor Terry Gibbs who banged his head on the pole while drunk and started giving a lecture to it. Since then, he has become a joke. 'Do not get drunk like Terry, or you gonna talk to the booth next as if it would hear ya.' But, please, I don't want any of that associated with my name, Olivia."

"I can understand, dear, I can understand. It's just that you will ruin yourself. You already have. Come on," Olivia stepped forward, took the books, grabbed Harry's hands, and almost dragged him out to the yard, "Go on, throw them now."

"But…"

"NO. NOW."

Harry looked at the top book and realized that Olivia was right; he could not let that incident get to his head and take away his peace.

Days passed, and he only got frustrated with

everything. He would usually stay quiet and leave early for work. He tried to focus on his job and keep himself busy, so he would not think about the incident. He also went for long jogs without breaks. He tried everything he could to make peace with the situation.

As a last resort, he went back to the place and to get slipped again. This was a desperate attempt to find answers to questions that had been keeping him up and were taking a toll on his mental health.

***

Charles was sitting in his office thinking about Harry and his case. He knew it was a 918, but for some unknown reason, he wanted to dig deeper. A moment ago, he was on a call with the famous Arnold James, the author of 'Time Collapsed Around Her.' The book was about how a man time-traveled to meet his wife, who died before their fifth anniversary. The novel ended with the man staying behind in the past, deciding to never return.

When Charles heard about the book, he searched everything regarding it and the author. Arnold had written articles about timeslips and even interviewed someone who claimed to have traveled through times. So, Charles called Arnold to talk about a few pointers that could help in Harry's case.

"I am sure you would have investigated deeply before writing the book?" Charles asked.

"Yes, I did. I interviewed a man who was the inspiration behind my main character for the book," Arnold replied.

"Oh, and did you believe what he told you?"

"Yes, because he went back to the middle ages, and I did find minute details which he told me. I was so shocked to see the truth, but there's always a possibility that he read the information somewhere and had a highly vivid dream."

"Yes, it could be the case. But, I am more interested in 'Powerless Against Time,' where you accounted for a few more incidents. Especially the one in England, where he slipped and found himself a year back in Wales."

"Oh, that was more of a fluke, I guess because when the incident happened, the person did go to Wales the previous year. So, it could have been a vivid dream. But, he was so frustrated and adamant about finding what was wrong with him. He was sure that he was telling the truth, but everyone kept calling him mad. But, I do have his number if you want to contact him?"

"Oh, it would frustrate anyone when you believe you are telling the truth and no one believes you. It's funny how this particular case has made me interact with English people, and it is quite an honor. But, I will pass on this opportunity because I've got enough information from the right source. Thank you so much for your precious time, Arnold."

"Hey, it is my pleasure. Feel free to contact me for anything. Good day, Charles."

The phone died, and Charles took a deep sigh. He knew that there was no smoking gun evidence to support why or how he slipped between times. Everything Harry had told Charles was the truth, but having no logical explanation for the incident frustrated him. He thought he might not have researched harder.

Charles looked at all his notes and went through all his resources one more time. He talked to his elders and understood the secrets of Gilberts from everyone he could. But, unfortunately, no one even remembered a rumor of how a modern man once ventured Gilbert in the 1900s

He even tried to dig deeper, but there was no recorded evidence of the value of Gilbert's town before the 1900s. After the last meeting with Harry, Charles knew that he would be frustrated and that motivated him to learn more and come to a logical conclusion. But nothing made sense anymore. The only thing Charles could tell Harry was that he believed him.

After a few days, Charles decided to call Harry and tell him about what was going on. He decided to keep the tone light and disclose the news with ease. Charles still wanted to dig deeper, but, as it seemed, there was nothing to look into anymore.

He picked his phone and dialed his number, but before he could hit the green button, his laptop pinged. The notification on the sidebar showed an email. It was from Harry. Putting aside his phone, he opened his mail and saw a message. He sighed and started reading,

"Charles,

I hope this mail finds you in good health.

I guess I am writing this message for the ninth time already. I wrote one message four days ago but could not send it. It is still in the drafts but, I am composing a new one as I've learned and am finally willing to accept that some things have no explanation. I've busied myself with work. I guess I'm trying to exhaust myself so I don't think about the incident anymore. I've become so mentally exhausted that I made a huge blunder at work.

This almost cost me my job, my genuine respect at the office. I've lost two clients to a stupid delivery mistake and ordered a shipment worth a thousand dollars that had nothing to do with my clients. There were mistakes in my paperwork, too, that flawed the company's reputation. But, after hanging on the line, I've retrieved myself enough to accept my mistakes, and my almost clean-slate record saved me from the ultimate doom.

I am grateful to have found you, Charles, as you're the only one who believed me. You have helped me look into this matter, and I know you have no solid evidence to support why or how I slipped back in time. I am frustrated that there is no answer but grateful that you went to the last means to retrieve it.

This incident has unhinged my wife and me, and I don't know what to think or feel anymore. However, I feel like a stupid punk who sleepwalked the streets of Gilbert, thinking I was way behind. Maybe that coyote was just a stray dog walking beside me. If you look at it from the angle of a delusion-induced dream or a hallucination, there can be theories on top of theories to support what happened. But, there is no solid evidence if we try to look for reasoning.

So, I want to ask you to stop this investigation as I am withdrawing from my case. I have transferred the amount to your bank, and this is a goodbye email. I have had enough of all this, and I would like to forget about it and move on for good.

I even told Olivia about my decision, and, though disappointed, she feels it is the best. She helped me throw away the books and delete the searches and bookmarks to help me move on.

Anyways, I would like to thank you, Charles, for your help. I am grateful to you and how you made sense of everything. I would be forever in your debt, for you were there when everyone gave up on me. This is Goodbye.

Good luck with your future cases. I hope they are not as hopeless as mine. Finally, I hope you have a wonderful life.

Harry."

Charles could not comprehend how he could suddenly withdraw from the case, but it was a relief as this was a time-consuming case with dead-ends at every corner.

He stood up, made himself a cup of coffee, and returned to his desk to finalize Harry's file and place it with the other 918 files when his phone rang. It was Olivia. Charles picked up and said, "Hi, Olivia."

"Hello, Charles. I hope you are well."

"Good, yes, but shocked."

"If you are shocked, you must have received Harry's mail. I was shocked for a while, too, because I thought he would want to pursue this for longer."

"Yes, I did receive his mail, and I felt the same

thing."

"I just called you to inform you that when I was helping him throw away some of the books, I saw the inscriptions he made. He explicitly wrote how he felt the desert around him. He even wrote how hungry he was when he entered the town and how some guy at the grocery store brought him food. I am just curious, if this was all a dream, how can he eat food and feel hungry?"

"I know, the grocery store was present in the Gilbert Archives, and even the information about the water tower. But, Olivia, even if Harry did time slip, there is no evidence or logical explanation of why and how it happened. Thus, we cannot come to any conclusion as to what is the right thing to say."

"I know, I believe him too now, but he should forget what happened. Poor man, cannot even sleep well."

"Yes, please do take care of him."

"Of course, and Charles, thank you so much for everything."

"Mention not. Stay blessed."

"You too. Goodbye."

Harry bid farewell and hung up the phone. He tried calling Harry next, but he did not answer the call. Everything was back to his place, and Charles knew Harry would not talk to him.

So, he gave up and went back to his everyday tasks. Charles was relieved to finally finish Harry's case and declare it a 918.

After a few days, looking at one of the local robbery cases, Charles received a call from his Aunt Christine. Of course, he was happy to answer it.

"Hi, Auntie."

"Charles, my boy. How have you been?"

"I am good, just a little busy. What about you?"

"Oh, you know, I am fine. Just a little back pain, but this lady ain't old."

"Haha, not a day older than eighteen."

"Alright, it's not that much young either. So, where has my favorite nephew been?"

"Oh, just here and there. In the present and the past. Closed my recent case a few days back and now, onto a new one."

"Oh, by chance, was that case one of your 918?"

"Yes, indeed it was."

"Oh, you know I love to hear about them."

"Yes, Auntie, you would love the details."

"Let me get my popcorns, dear."

As Charles settled back to tell everything to Christine about Harry's story, his laptop pinged again.

He ignored everything and concentrated on telling her everything about the case. It was always fun to talk to her about such cases because she gave her insight and loved talking crazy. Finally, after a long call, Charles bade goodbye with a promise of calling her again soon.

He went back to his work and checked his emails before they stacked upon him and made his workplace and mind clutter. The first few went to the trash bin instantly as they were about insurance and utility funds. The next few were asking for updates about what happened with their cases.

Charles laughed as a few of them had been finished long ago but, people still need more. Scrolling through the tiresome but essential work, he came across an email that was from a man up in Payson.

After a quick overview of what the mail contained, he was interested in the particular case. He hit reply and wrote,

"Mr. Kaminsky,

I received your mail and would like to find out more details about this case. You have described that some of your horses and cattle at the ranch farm are getting killed but, there seems to be no motive. You even asked me what I think, and I cannot suggest anything for I don't have enough information yet. However, I would like to invite you to contact me as you have not given any other contact details to discuss the matter further.

Thank you for contacting me, and I look forward to discussing this further.

Thank you,

Charles G. William

Zona Investigations"

Sending the reply, Charles sat back, took a sip of coffee, and said, "now, let's hope this one isn't a 918."

918

"This went on for a while. Although Harry's withdrawal from the case meant it was no longer a case." So, Charles did what he could; he wrote the report for his official business and closed the file. And like that, Charles moved on toward other cases that had been waiting in the list of Zona Investigations.

Still finding it hard to believe, Brady asked Charles, "Grandpa, you must have kept some other proofs regarding what happened to Harry or the case."

"I did not, my son. I had other cases that needed my attention. So, I moved on and let the memory of Harry's case rest in the back of my head."

Hoping to add meaning to this case, his grandson inquired further on, "Okay, there were a lot of proofs, but what if he was lying? Did Harry get to time travel again, grandpa? Because if that was the truth, Harry must have been able to time travel again. Did he say anything?"

"Maybe he did, maybe he did not. I guess we will never know. I never tried to contact him since that one time I called him after listening to his message in the mail. About Harry lying, as far as all the proofs said, he was surely not lying."

"How are you so sure of it?"

"You see, my son, working in the Air Force and as a detective, made me very keen on details. I always saw things differently than other human beings. It was not like I had been sure about Harry's story since the beginning, but when I skimmed through so much paper and pieces of information, it was clear that Harry had not made up the story."

"I have so many stories where I can make anyone believe that I can become a robotic car if I want to. My friends fall for it every time, and they are always so surprised; they think I transform every night, help people, and keep the city safe. So, what if Harry wanted his friends to be shocked?"

Charles couldn't suppress it longer and laughed a little at his little yet fierce Brady's attempt to approach the case with an adult perspective. However, he was failing; it made him realize that Brady's curiosity and close observation blended into one cup would make him an outstanding detective one day.

A look at his grandson's face brought Charles back from his thoughts; he had an eagerness to know about the rest of the details. Charles continued,

"First of all, you shouldn't be lying to your friends even if you want to amaze them. There are different ways to stun your friends, okay? Secondly, if I did not believe his words like the rest of the world, how would I have known whether or not he was telling the truth? This is why being a detective means looking into stuff closely and not missing any dot, and believing everything your client tells you until you can prove otherwise."

"Ohhh... Did you get scared, grandpa? What if there were aliens?"

"Your old man might seem weak because of these white strands on his head, but he is not. Whenever I was working on a case, I was fearless. Some cases baffled me, just like Gilbert00017 but never scared me. And aliens? I have many stories in that category too, son."

"Aliens? I have always wanted to know more and more about aliens. Did Harry get to meet aliens when he time traveled?"

"No, he did not because I don't think aliens are that easy to find. I will tell you more about these cases some other day."

"Grandpa," he paused. "Do you think Harry would have been able to get out if he got stuck in between this world and the place where he time-traveled to?"

"No, Brady, he couldn't have gotten stuck in the first place. There is no place in between. There is past, present, and future. He left, and then he came back."

"If I were in your place, I would not have believed Harry, especially without proofs."

"Brady, my son, always remember that when you are in the same field as I am, you have to believe people until you find valid proof otherwise. Who would have believed Harry if I didn't? If I had not looked more into the case, I wouldn't be here telling you this story."

"I guess you are right. Mom always says that I should

stay in one place and think with a calming mind. Maybe if I think from a calming mind, I will understand what Harry was trying to say."

Brady was staring at the wall while saying, "What if this was a plan to get you to the aliens, grandpa?"

"It was not a plan."

"So, Harry did not want his friends to be amazed because he could time travel?"

"No, my son. Something happened to him, and he tried his best to find answers. But some things are better left untouched."

"What things? Did Harry see something else? Why did he need answers? You said it yourself; Harry was scared after this incident."

Brady's questions puzzled Charles. The extent his grandson was ready to reach just to put his always intrigued mind at ease. For a third-grader, Brady's mind worked differently.

"No, my handsome little man," Charles stated, caressing Brady's hair. "Harry did not see anything unusual.

He saw an old version of the city. He saw people nowhere near how he had seen people all his life. He needed answers because he was confused, son. Just like you are asking me questions right now because you are confused. Similarly, he came to me, looking for answers. So, I could help him understand what happened and whether or not it was real."

He stood up, squealing with excitement, "Can we go and meet Harry?"

"I don't know his address, and besides, why would you want to go to his place?"

"Okay," Brady said with a sad tone, "but what did you mean when you said some things are left untouched? You did not answer this."

This was the moment when Charles realized it had gone too far.

"Brady, your mom is looking for you. Go, see what she wants. We will continue this later."

Charles knew this was the only way to divert his attention, and to his surprise, Brady actually ran out of the room without asking him a million more questions. Charles now had the space to himself and complete silence.

Talking about the 918 was fun with Brady, and no doubt, he was a remarkable child and understood more than any other kid Charles had ever known, but some things are just not for a child's mind.

Every human being has something special in life that stays close to their heart. The 918 files were that part of Charles' life. There were days when he thought maybe he was not good enough for this business, but remembering all the cases that he had worked on made him realize how perfect he was for this place.

There were so many people waiting to be heard. So many cases were significant, but they were never looked into due to lack of evidence. When Charles started working individually, he had one motto: to help the unheard. It seemed cliché to some people, but only Charles knew how many files were stored in boxes covered with dust. He knew the evidence was essential, but it was not as crucial as the troubled brain of someone desperate to be heard.

He used to wonder what goes on in these peoples' minds. They're telling the truth most of the time, at least the truth as they see it, but nobody believes them. He could only imagine how it felt not to have your family by your side when you need them the most.

Charles worked day and night to connect the dots just so he would not even mistakenly leave a shred of evidence unnoticed. It got out of his hands sometimes, and during that time, his wife was the one who dragged him out of his office and reminded him that a family was waiting outside of the world he had created with those files; Gilbert00017 was one of them.

Gilbert00017 opened his eyes to a world that remained unseen to many. However, a part of Charles was relieved that Harry took back the case, but a part of him also had this unsettling feeling that made him want to find out exactly what happened. Harry remembered so many details to prove his words, and he did. Although they were not enough for the law to believe him, they were sufficient for Charles to believe everything he had said.

Charles found himself thinking about Harry many times even after the case closed. He could not help but think maybe if he had worked more into it, he might have been able to find a reliable lead. It is not like Charles did not find any information; he did. He found information that made him believe he was very close to the destination, but then again, after a few days, he stood there wrong and headed toward a dead end every time. Charles wondered what must be going on in Harry's mind right now? Charles knew it was anything but easy to forget what happened and move on simply. What about Harry's family? Because Charles knew he was still thinking about it even though it had been years.

He snapped out of his thoughts when another box filled with his old files fell on the ground. He knew he would miss this - the mixture of feelings when he started looking into the details of the case and the happiness of achieving something. Moreover, the look on the client's face when he assured them that they weren't crazy. The feeling of contentment when he gave them the answers they were looking for.

"Dad? Is everything okay? I thought I heard something." Charles's daughter, Lily, entered the room with a worried look on her face.

"Yeah, nothing serious. The box fell, I..." He didn't

even get to finish his sentence when she came rushing to where he was standing.

"Oh, Good Lord! Dad, are you hurt? This is why I asked Brady to help you and stay with you. Let's get you seated first."

It was at that moment that Charles realized he had lived a good life. A beautiful family, a perfect wife, and unbelievably sweet children. He got the chance to follow his dreams and to achieve all of his goals.

"Yes, Lily. I'm alright, don't worry. Brady was here with me for the most part; I just had to send him away for a while. We don't want him digging into all of this old man's secrets, huh?" Charles completed his sentence smiling with a wink.

"So… What is this 918 stuff Brady is so excited about?"

"It is nothing much, ju- just an old case I had told him about."

"Dad? I told you not to tell him more about these things. You know how he gets, right?"

193

"It was not anything huge. I was sharing some of the best cases I have had."

"Ahaan, dad, then what was this one about?"

"My dear, it was an old case. This guy came up to me and told me how he time-traveled to a city and how everything was so strange. When he returned and told his family about it, nobody seemed to believe him, which is why he came to me and asked for help."

Lily huffed. Charles knew something was coming, "Dad." Ahh! There it was. "Don't you think that this was too much to be true? Time-traveling dad, seriously?"

"I know it is hard for you to believe, but I had legit pieces of evidence to prove my statement, but they weren't precisely legit to use it as proof to show them to someone else. That is why we had to close the case. The details were a bit rough, but that was the truth. When I tell you I had evidence, I mean it."

Lily's facial expressions changed for a second, which made Charles think she almost believed it but then it was back to normal, "I don't know, Dad, I am still not sure if these things are to be taken seriously."

"This is just a page of the book of series of unusual things I have seen. I have had cases where UFOs or some weird creatures were involved. That is a story for another time."

There was a pause before she continued, "I am just glad you are okay though; you scared me, you know?" Lily said with a sad smile.

"Well, it is safe to say that you won't have to worry about me for too long. I will have people to look after me in the nursing home."

"Dad, you know I am doing this for you. I can't let you live alone after mom."

"I know my child; I'm blessed to have you here." Lily hugged him with tears in her eyes.

"Uhh- come on, where is your son? Tell him to come and help this old man." Their laughter echoed in the house, followed by the sound of Brady's footsteps approaching them.

"There he is," said Lily.

"Grandpa! Grandpa! I told mom about Harry, but she won't believe me. Tell her about him, tell her pleaseee."

"We can tell her the whole story later, right now, little man, you have to help me pack."

***

"Are you going to get rid of these files, grandpa?"

"I thought I would do that, but I don't think I will. They are not just files; they are a part of my life." This is why I decided to take all of these files with me. It would be a hassle to pack all of them and take them along, but these cases are worth the hassle."

"Hmm," said Brady, "Do we have to keep all of the clothes in one suitcase, grandpa?"

Charles nodded, to which Brady replied, "But they won't fit in here. The suitcase is too small for your clothes."

"No, it's not. Wait. Here, let me show you how to fold these and fit them here."

"I will miss you, grandpa. I will miss staying with you."

"Well, you can still come and stay with me when mom goes shopping."

"YES! And I want you to tell me about some other case the next time when I meet you."

It was almost 7:30 pm when Charles and Brady got done packing and started putting boxes out in the lounge. This house had all of its memories stored into its depths, which made leaving harder, but Charles knew he could come back and sit here for as long as he wanted to, making it a little better.

This was the place where Charles decided he would start working individually; this was the office where he had spent so many sleepless nights trying to solve case after case. Charles could finally sit in a chair in front of a garden and think about all the people he helped through his work.

It is not easy to serve and protect. Everyone has a sense of compassion in their hearts, but people who enter such career paths have a higher sense of duty and the will to protect others. Charles was meant to become a private investigator and see what others couldn't even comprehend. He had spent his life knowing what other people would never know, which made him grateful for the work he had done.

Epilogue

June 2019...Cheyenne, Wyoming...Mrs. Walden, an 80-year-old woman, sat in her wooden rocking chair waiting for her grandson, Ron.

His grandmother had been living alone ever since the passing of her husband, which was why Ron made sure that he would come to visit once a week. He knew his grandma loved his company because she had been very lonely after grandpa's death.

"Grandmaaa, look who is back!" Ron screamed with excitement as he entered the house through the back door and found his grandmother cooking in the kitchen. Grandma smiled and hugged him back, "What a pleasant surprise! I thought you were coming tomorrow?"

"I figured I'd stop by early, and what's even better, I'm here for the weekend. Ron said with a big smile on his face.

"Well, you're in luck; I just finished making dinner,

so come on, let's eat. I have so much stuff that I need to tell you."

They both had dinner and talked about Ron's new job till the late hours of the night.

The next morning, Mrs. Walden placed a box full of old photo albums on the table in front of her grandson because she knew how much he loved going through old photographs and knowing more and more about family history.

"Hey, grandma. What is this?" he picked up the picture and showed it to Mrs. Walden, "Ohh, mann! is this a coyote?" asked Ron with excitement and confusion leaking his tone.

"What is it? I'm not sure where it came from." Mrs. Walden added with the same confusion.

"It is a black and white photo of a coyote in the desert. One of the front paws looks bright white... I wonder if it's actually white or did the camera mess up?" continued Ron while looking at his grandmother, hoping he helped her remember.

"Oh, I remember this photo," Grandma narrated the story to Ron, "It belongs to my grandfather. I remember he used to tell us this story all the time. We were little, and every time he mentioned this coyote photograph, he'd get so excited, and so would my siblings and me since he told the story in a way only a grandpa could tell it.

Grandfather had seen a Coyote with a white paw while doing land surveying work in Arizona during the summer. No, it was not the camera. It was the paw. The white paw of that coyote was so odd to him that he took a picture of it."

"Where did he even see this thing? What was he doing in the desert?" asked Ron with curiosity.

"I don't know. He said it just appeared in front of him out of nowhere. Grandfather used to work as a surveyor during summer as part of his job."

Mrs. Walden continued telling her grandson about how this story was her grandfather's favorite. It came up every time the photo albums came out, which was a lot.

"That is so cool," he flipped the photograph and then

read the words written on the back, "Phoenix Arizona Area Circa 1918."

"Yes, it has been so long," Mrs. Walden said, looking out of the window, deep in her thoughts.

"Man, 1918, this photo is old... so cool," Ron said while he placed it down back in the box and put it aside.